DIRTBIKE
DAREDEVILS

Pam Withers

Text copyright © 2006 by Pam Withers
Walrus Books
A Division of Whitecap Books Ltd.

Second Printing 2008

Edited by Carolyn Bateman
Proofread by Joan Templeton
Cover and interior design by Roberta Batchelor
Cover photograph © picturesbyrob / Alamy
Typeset by Michelle Mayne

Printed and bound in Canada

Library and Archives Canada Cataloguing in Publication

Withers, Pam
    DirtBike Daredevils / Pam Withers.
(Take it to the extreme)
ISBN 1-55285-804-9
ISBN 978-1-55285-804-2

    I. Title. II. Series: Withers, Pam Take it to the extreme.
PS8595.I8453D57 2006   jC813'.6   C2006-900698-9

The publisher acknowledges the support of the Canada Council for the Arts and the Cultural Services Branch of the Government of British Columbia for our publishing program. We acknowledge the financial support of the Government of Canada through the Book Publishing Industry Development Program for our publishing activities.

ANCIENT FOREST
FRIENDLY

The inside pages of this book are 100% recycled, processed chlorine-free paper with 40% post-consumer content. For more information, visit Markets Initiative's website: www.oldgrowthfree.com.

DIRTBIKE
DAREDEVILS

To the Lawrence family

Contents

1	Back of Beyond	1
2	Dana	7
3	The Ranch House	15
4	Freestyle Tricks	29
5	The Llamas	40
6	Dirt Trails	47
7	Sidehilling	61
8	Spokane	71
9	Moto	79
10	Second Heat	92
11	Whoops	105
12	Upper Trail	118
13	The Lake	127
14	Stakeout	136
15	Lower Trail	147
16	Losing Sergei	157
17	Rain	165
18	Hero	176
19	Mud	185
20	The Cabin	194
21	To the Rescue	204
22	The Dig	217
23	Clients	228
24	The Team	232
	Acknowledgements	246
	About the Author	251

1   Back of Beyond

The crack of a rifle shot woke Jake Evans with a start. He sat straight up in bed. *Thunk!* His head hit the undersides of the cramped trailer's bunk bed above.

"What was that?" The alarmed voice from above belonged to his best friend Peter Montpetit, who seemed to rock the entire trailer as he sat up in his bunk. Both threw off their covers and scrambled to the trailer's single window. The cold linoleum of the floor against Jake's bare feet made him shiver. The greasy smell of last night's burgers assaulted his nostrils from an unwashed frying pan in the tiny sink.

A full moon lit the entire expanse of the remote, 150-acre ranch. It silhouetted nearby bluffs. It illuminated tall evergreens waving gently across distant sheep fields. It made the dew-heavy grass shimmer around the full-sized motocross track sitting fifty yards from the boys' trailer door.

Jake moved his glance toward the ranch house, where an upstairs light had appeared. Then his eye caught movement in the farm sheds near the house. The moonlight played on the faces of the ranch's three male llamas, which had emerged ears up and faces alert.

"That shot came from right near the llama shed, but look at them," Jake said, running a hand through his thick brown hair. "Calm and curious, as if rifles go off in the middle of the night all the time."

"They're sure not like the sheep out in the far field," Peter agreed. "They're running in circles. Can you see anything, Jake?"

"There's Sergei," Jake replied, pointing to a burly figure stepping out the front door of the ranch house in his pajamas. The young ranch owner carried his rifle in one hand and was patting Scout, the ranch's border collie, on the head with his other.

"Maybe a coyote was threatening the lambs?" Peter guessed.

"Nah, that's what Hero, the guard llama, is for. Sergei says if Hero catches a coyote near the sheep flock, he'll kick the coyote most of the way to Spokane."

"Spokane?" Peter laughed. "That's 100 miles away. Remind me never to get on a llama's bad side."

They watched Sergei Dobrynina amble across the rutted driveway to the front lawn of the ranch house. He stooped and picked up something limp and white.

"He got a rabbit," Jake said, shaking his head incredulously.

"From his bedroom window at four in the morning, just for fun," Peter added, rolling his eyes. "What a weird guy."

"Hey, he's Russian. They do things differently," Jake said, shrugging and climbing back into bed. "How normal do you expect someone to be who grew up on a farm in Russia, became a motocross champion, then studied to become a veterinarian?"

"Yeah, must've been tough to go through the hoops to immigrate to the US, then have them refuse to recognize his vet degree," Peter finished for him. "So he rents a bunch of land in the boonies of eastern Washington, builds a dirt-bike track, and tries to make a living."

"Tries? I think he's doing it. Otherwise we wouldn't be here," Jake pointed out.

Peter shuffled over to the bunk beds in his boxers and sprang up to his mattress in one leap.

"Hey!" Jake complained. "Way to nearly crack the bunk and make it land on my head."

Peter's head of messy blond curls appeared upside

down with a grin. "So, you think Sergei is going to make a living here in nowhere land?"

"Sure," Jake replied, rearranging his pillow under his head and pulling his quilt up to his chin. "He's got 100 sheep, so he sells lambs. And he's got llamas for backcountry llama-cart rides."

"That earns him peanuts," Peter objected, withdrawing his head from view. "Dana told me."

Jake wondered if Dana Young, Sergei's fifteen-year-old farm helper, really knew. She knew animals, that's for sure, being a local farmer's kid herself. And she rode a pretty mean dirt bike in her off-hours, which is why she liked her summer job with Back-of-Beyond Ranch.

"Sergei will do fine," Jake said, yawning. "He was smart enough to contact Sam's Adventure Tours, so now he's one of Sam's outfitters. And Sam was impressed enough to send us here. We're Sam's favorite junior guides, so it must look promising."

Peter's mop of curls appeared again, and his voice adopted a deep, dramatic tone as he quoted from the new brochure. "Sam's Adventure Tours introduces llama-cart rides and off-road dirt-bike tours at a large ranch in eastern Washington state. A mechanic tunes up clients' bikes daily and accompanies them on tours …"

"That's me!" Jake said proudly, then muttered,

"With a little help from Sergei."

"…Dirt-bike guides select trails with panoramic views on a variety of terrain suited to each client's skills and taste," Peter continued in his mock bass voice, then switched to a lighter tone: "That's me, with a little help from Sergei."

Together they finished off the brochure from memory: "Enjoy comfortable ranch-house quarters and delicious home cooking."

Jake snorted. "*Clients*, that is. Lowly fifteen-year-old guides and mechanics will share a stuffy trailer, suffer their own lousy cooking, and get woken up in the middle of the night by crazy, rabbit-shooting Russians."

"Oh, stop complaining," Peter said, flopping about as he tried to get comfortable again in his bunk. "It's not like Sam's Adventure Tours headquarters has a motocross track for when we get off work. And the use of ten bikes: two 250cc's, six 125s, and two 80s."

"True," Jake allowed as his eyelids grew heavy.

"And two motocross fanatics good for some hot coaching tips. Even if one of them hardly ever says anything to us."

Jake's foggy brain decided Peter meant Dana. "She's shy," he rose to Dana's defence. "Sergei told us first thing that she's more comfortable around animals than people. Why is that weird? She's a farm girl who grew up on a llama farm. We're city kids who arrived two days ago. She doesn't know us. You can't blame her for not talking to us more than she has to."

"Yeah, well I'm steering clear of her. Of her dirt bike, too. She rides like a crazy girl."

"You're just jealous, Peter. She's a motocross racer. And you're crazier 'cause you do backflips. Or claim you've done one, anyway."

Peter's head appeared once more, his white teeth gleaming in the moonlight as he delivered a wide grin. "Jake, I'm a freestyle maniac. You're jealous. Get over it already."

Jealous? That would be the day, Jake thought. "You're a maniac, anyway," he allowed. "And I'm going to be a sleep-deprived maniac if you don't shut up. Go to sleep, Peter!" He lifted his feet for a moment to deliver a gentle kick to Peter's sagging form through the mattress.

"Hey, it was that Russian maniac who woke us up, not me. But okay. Good night, old buddy."

2   Dana

Jake's eyelids were wrenched open again a few hours later by the sound of a dirt bike gunning it on the track in front of their trailer. He opened one eye and registered that it was daylight.

"Dana," Peter groaned overhead. "Doesn't that girl know how to sleep in on a Sunday morning? Or be noisy somewhere else on this ranch?"

"Farm girls don't sleep in," Jake reasoned as he rolled over, wide awake now. "Especially when they're training for Saturday's race in Spokane."

Although he and Peter had been on the ranch less than two days, Jake already had the dirt-bike jargon down. A "moto" was a heat of a motocross race, where dirt bikes raced around a track featuring bulldozer-sculpted humps of dirt—some of them six feet high—between rutted stretches of road called straightaways. A race usually consisted of two motos.

Despite the heavy workload Sergei had assigned the boys to prepare for the new dirt-bike trail tours, they'd already spent a couple of hours a day of their free time polishing their motocross skills on Sergei's course. Yesterday Sergei had talked them into entering the Spokane motocross race on Saturday. But even with the ranch owner's coaching, Jake wasn't sure he was ready.

He wasn't like Peter, who'd raced for three years and spent two weeks the previous summer at a motocross camp. That experience had helped him perfect everything from "getting the holeshot" (getting out of the starting gate and into the first corner in first place) to performing freestyle tricks. Peter had returned totally into the freestyle stuff, which pretty much freaked Jake. Peter scoffed at him for it, but Jake preferred the pits. He was like his dad: a natural-born mechanic who liked fiddling with the innards of a machine way more than riding it. Without a skilled mechanic, Jake figured, a dirt bike was just a jumble of parts trying to communicate with one another. With Jake's touch, a dirt bike sang like an angel. Bikes *he* tuned up certainly didn't sound like Dana's did now; he could hear it coughing on a turn this very moment. He knew without even looking at it that it needed jetting: a carburetor adjustment.

Of course, bike mechanics could ride, too. How

else would they learn how to make a bike run well? Jake figured he could survive a moto; he wouldn't finish last or anything. But the truth was, racing didn't excite him as much as working on racers' bikes.

"That's enough!" Peter's shout disturbed Jake's thoughts. "She's driving me crazy!" He leapt out of bed and yanked open the trailer's door.

"Enough already!" he shouted in Dana's direction, prompting her to turn her head his way. He gestured for Dana to come talk to him. Jake grinned as his friend's T-shirt and boxers ruffled in the doorway breeze.

"Dana!" Peter shouted above the whine of her bike.

Jake rose to look out the window. Judging by the way she turned her head and nodded, Dana had caught Peter's request. She responded by accelerating up a tabletop—a hill with a flattened top—and sailing over its plateau. While suspended in midair, she lifted herself a little off her seat and brought her legs up high like a horse rider about to give a heavy kick to her horse's sides. But as Jake raised an arm to shade his eyes from the sun, those legs kept coming up and forward until—hands still tight on her handlebars—she'd wrapped her legs around her elbows and clicked her boots' heels together. Whoa, he thought. Quite the contortionist's trick. He watched, open-mouthed, as Dana casually dropped her feet back to either side of her seat and returned them to her foot pegs just in time for a perfect landing on the downward slope of the dirt pile.

"That was a Heel Clicker," Peter informed Jake. As if Jake didn't know that from watching Peter's free-style motocross videos. "It's the easiest freestyle trick. She can't do a Superman Seat-Grab or a backflip." Peter sounded a little defensive to Jake.

Jake watched Dana motor down the tabletop, leave the track, and point her 125cc toward their trailer door. He left the window and began tugging jeans on. Peter might not care, but Jake wasn't going to let Dana see him in his boxers.

"Think she might take the freestyle purse this weekend?" Jake asked as he finished dressing. That would get Peter going. "Sergei says there's $100 to be won during the halftime freestyle show."

"Not if I can grab it," Peter declared.

"Not if you can grab what?" came a soft female voice as Dana cut the motor on her bike and removed her goggles.

"Grab a sleep-in on a Sunday morning," Peter said, crossing his arms as he looked down on her from the trailer's doorway. "You have all day to do the course. Can't you train later and let us junior guides sleep in?"

Dana lifted her helmet off her short, thick black

curls and rested it in the crook of her arm. Her face was moist with sweat. Her eyes flicked up to Peter's face before they glued themselves to her handlebars. During the two days they'd been on the ranch, she'd hardly said a word to them. Sergei had told them she was excessively shy. "She only talks if you ask her about one of two things: llamas or motocross," he'd said. Then he'd shrugged. "Crazy girl, but the best llama handler I've ever met."

Dana was resting her steel-tipped motocross boots on the dusty ground in front of the trailer. Her motocross jersey and matching riding pants clung to her small, muscled frame in the morning heat. Slowly she removed her gloves and tucked them between her plastic chest protector, which resembled hockey armor, and her light blue jersey.

"Sorry, Peter, but I have to train before it's time to take Furball out." Furball was the young male llama she was training, a llama Sergei referred to as "a pack of trouble, a real devil."

"Does Furball know morning from afternoon?" Peter sneered. "If you took him out now, we could sleep. Then you could train on the course later."

Jake couldn't imagine going back to sleep at this point. And he thought Peter didn't need to be so rude to the farmhand.

Dana shook her head like a teacher amused with

a child. But she spoke more softly than a teacher and wouldn't look directly at them. "Furball knows the day's routine to the minute, and he has to stick to a schedule or there's big trouble."

That was a real mouthful of words for the quiet girl, Jake reflected. He wanted to ask what kind of trouble. He'd heard that angry llamas could dislocate a person's shoulder if they head-butted them. He wanted to know why Furball was a "devil."

But Peter obviously wasn't interested in the ranch's llamas. "Well, anyway, Jake, Sergei, and I are running the course this afternoon. Join us if you like. It'd be more like a real moto with all four of us."

Jake grinned inwardly. Hadn't Peter said last night she was too crazy a rider to share a course with? The truth is Peter is thinking he can pick up some technique from her.

Dana's mouth tugged into a shy half-smile as she studied the helmet in her lap. "I'm training in the pool this afternoon."

"The *pool*?" Jake heard himself ask in the same astonished tone as Peter. He stepped into full view in the small trailer's doorway, prompting Dana to lift her head.

"The pool behind the ranch house," she said, shifting her body on the dirtbike's seat. "You haven't seen it?"

"No way!" Peter responded. "Sergei didn't tell us he had a swimming pool."

"He doesn't," she said, tossing her head to shake curls out of her dark eyes, which sparkled for a moment. "He's only renting the farm, but even if he owned it, he'd be too cheap to fix up and fill the pool. He's Sergei. He thinks swimming pools and Americans are outrageously extravagant."

"Dana, what are you talking about?" Peter demanded.

"My pool. He let me have it, so I filled it with blocks of foam from old mattresses."

Jake scratched his head as his buddy fell silent.

"No way!" Peter finally burst out excitedly. "They had one like that at my motocross camp! So that's where you practised your Heel Clicker? Perfect! I mean ..." he piped down and swung the trailer door open wider, "can Jake and I try it out? I'd love to practise my backflip before the race on Saturday," he added, pulling himself up tall.

Dana was silent for a few seconds. "Jake?" she asked at length.

"Yeah," Jake replied, stepping out from behind Peter and wishing Dana would stop fiddling with her throttle. She was going to flood the carburetor.

"My bike's running a bit rough. I've tried cleaning the air filter and changing the spark plug, but it's still spluttering. If you're willing to have a look at it, I'll show you and Peter the pool. The two of you can practise moves there if you want."

"Sure, I'll look at your bike," Jake said, puffing up his chest. He'd do it even though he had no intention of using the pool. Accelerating a dirt bike up a ramp, catching air, and landing in a swimming pool full of foam pieces was crazy. In fact, he hoped he could persuade Peter not to do it, either. Freestyle was dangerous, and backflips were insane. Peter would end up getting hurt, which would leave Jake to do all the work on the ranch. Sergei and Sam would be furious. What was Peter thinking?

Dana lifted her helmet back onto her head and checked her watch. "See you at two o'clock behind the ranch house, then. You can use my toolbox, Jake."

"Mine's better," Jake replied. Way, way better, he reflected proudly as the girl nodded, kicked her bike into action, and tore away.

3   The Ranch House

Peter raced through the morning's chores, hardly able to contain his excitement. Imagine not noticing the pool behind Sergei and Natalia's ranch house! Then again, two days wasn't a lot for exploring a 150-acre piece of land. That was 150 acres butting onto Forest Service land, which gave Sergei lots of rugged trails to run both his trail-bike tours and llama-cart rides. This place was awesome, Peter reflected. A sweet vacation from his crowded Seattle neighborhood, where it rained too much even in the summer. Today's discovery of the pool was a major bonus. Plus, Sergei had been giving him some great tips for motocross racing.

Even without the motocross course and pool, Peter considered the ranch the perfect place to spend his summer. And he was getting paid to do it, with his best friend around for company! He could hardly wait to help guide an overnight trip to the Forest Service's A-frame cabin Sergei had permission to use. It sat on a bluff an hour and a half's ride away. Some gnarly trails connected here to there: rutted tracks along narrow trails with cliffs on one side and drop-offs on the other.

But to Peter's mind, here was the very strangest thing about Back-of-Beyond Ranch: every day, Dana harnessed three llamas up to a funny little cart and took them for workouts along the trails. The same trails Jake and Peter loved to speed their dirt bikes along, those llamas pulled her along at full speed: up to twenty miles per hour. No horse or donkey would go near those trails, let alone *fly* along them with a cart and driver. She was a madwoman, that Dana. Like a stagecoach driver out of a western, except that the cart was hardly larger than a wide snowmobile or Jet Ski. It was basically a plank with backrest over large wheels, wide enough for a driver and one or two passengers. The trio of llamas who pulled it like a chariot were pony-sized, shaggy-coated things with long necks and legs, rabbit-like ears, huge eyes, and long eyelashes. Could anyone blame Peter for wanting to pet them now and again? They were totally exotic!

Sergei had told Jake and Peter that some llama farms in these parts even ran llama cart races. Yes, races on these crazy trails. How cool was that?

"Peter!" Sergei's deep, booming voice broke into Peter's reverie as he swept out the dusty garage where the dirt bikes were kept.

"Yes, Sergei?" Peter paused and turned to see the husky Russian ranch owner standing in the sunlit doorway.

"Natalia says you and Jake can come eat lunch in the ranch house. She says she needs your opinion on her rabbit stew and poppyseed bread."

Peter raised the broom in a victory salute. "Alright! We'll be there right away, Sergei. Thanks!"

The big man smiled and disappeared. Peter tossed the broom in a corner and sprinted for the door. He jogged past the henhouse, pausing just long enough to lean over the wood railing and level a "cock-a-doodle-doo" at the rooster nearby. The rooster rushed at him, flapping its wings and shaking its red comb.

"Nah-nah, Rocky the Rooster, you're not fast enough," he taunted it.

"Jake!" he cried as his buddy narrowly avoided crashing into him. Jake was backing out of the chicken coop with an armful of eggs. "Watch where you're going!"

"Me watch where *I'm* going? I'm the one carrying eggs here," Jake challenged crossly. "What's the rush, anyway?"

"Natalia is trying out recipes again, and we get to

be food testers. That's my favorite job, for sure!" Peter grinned. Sergei's wife loved to cook, and now that the couple was hoping for an army of llama-cart and dirt-bike customers, she'd been reading cookbooks and testing recipes like someone studying for an exam.

"Not cabbage soup again?" Jake asked, making a face.

"Cabbage soup is called borscht, and her borscht is not bad," Peter informed him. "But today it's rabbit stew and poppyseed bread."

Jake shrugged. "Okay, beats your peanut butter and jelly sandwiches." He eased his eggs into a basket and joined Peter up the pathway to the ranch house.

"Boys!" Sergei greeted them as he scraped some chairs back from the long wooden table and reached a hand out to take Jake's basket. He was dressed as always in black tracksuit pants, army-style boots, and an odorous, threadbare T-shirt. He looked closer to thirty-five than his thirty years. Thick sideburns and bushy eyebrows glistened with sweat, and his breath smelled of tobacco. But his weathered face accommodated a wide smile. "You like rabbit stew? I shot him last night."

"Smells delicious," Peter said, rubbing his hands and beaming at Natalia. Her black-glossed lips formed a smile as long, polished nails reached up to push her waist-length black hair over her shoulders.

"Americans like rabbit stew, yes?" she asked him as she donned a chef's apron over the well-toned tummy, which peeked out between hip-hugging jeans and a skimpy cotton blouse. Dangling, fake-diamond earrings danced from her earlobes. "And you think they like poppyseed bread, maybe?" Her blue eyes, in startling contrast to long, dark lashes, searched Peter's before she turned back to the stove. Her high-heeled sandals tapped their way toward the kitchen's big stove.

While Peter was contemplating an answer, she pulled on some oven mitts and yanked on the handle of the oven door. "Eeeeeii!" she cried as the mitts rose above her bony, tanned shoulders. "The bread, it is fallen."

"Fallen?" Peter asked, scratching his head.

"Not risen properly," Sergei explained with a wink at the boys.

"This oven, she is not good!" Natalia wailed as she reached in and brought out a dense-looking loaf. Her pretty face was so grave you'd think someone needed to phone 911, Peter mused.

Peter didn't care what the bread looked like. It smelled good enough to eat all in one swallow. "Natalia, it smells perfect," he protested as his mouth watered. "You're the greatest."

She turned and gazed at him, face flushed from

the kitchen's heat, arms buried to her elbows in the oversized oven mitts. "You are good boy," she said, clucking her tongue and flapping her arms. For a second, she reminded Peter of Rocky the Rooster. Or a *Glamour* fashion model imitating a rooster's movements.

"Yes, we will eat anyway," she decided. "Next time I make better. American clients like bigger bread, yes?"

"Americans like everything big," Sergei suggested, lowering his bushy eyebrows and surveying the boys. Though he retained a heavy Russian accent, he spoke English fluently.

"The clients will love you, Natalia," Peter reassured her as he reached to pull a piece of steaming bread from the first slice she cut from the loaf.

Sergei's calloused hands lifted a ladle from a drawer and dropped it into the pot of stew on the table.

"*Priyatnava appeteeta*, or bon appétit," he declared with a broad smile. "This rabbit, he died for a good cause!"

"Thanks, Sergei and Natalia," Jake spoke up politely. "What about Dana? Isn't she joining us?"

Peter watched Natalia remove her oven mitts, shake her head, and wring her hands. "Dana, *nyet*. Always *nyet*. This girl, she needs to eat." She shot a worried look at her husband, who shrugged.

"Dana can look after herself," he declared, smothering

a piece of bread with butter.

"But she forgets sometimes, and then it is trouble ..." Natalia arched her plucked eyebrows and shot her husband a pleading look.

"Stop worrying about Dana," Sergei ruled, reaching over to take one of Natalia's hands in his. Then he said something in Russian to her, which prompted her to glance furtively at the boys, as if fearful they might have understood whatever he said.

As busy as Peter was ladling some of the rabbit stew into his bowl, he had a feeling Sergei was chiding his wife for nearly revealing some information she wasn't supposed to. Then again, since Peter didn't understand a word of Russian, why would he think that?

"Excellent stew," Peter complimented Natalia. "Anytime you need an opinion on what Americans like to eat, or whether a dish has turned out okay, just let me know."

Natalia released a girlish giggle and patted Peter's head before accepting the chair that Sergei had pulled out for her.

"They like filled pools too, yes, Peter?" she asked, tossing her hair and glancing flirtatiously at her husband. "If Sergei fills pool, I can sunbathe beside it like on television show *Dallas*, *da*? This is why we come to America, Sergei."

"Someday it will be your *Dallas* pool, Natalia!" Sergei teased her back, winking at the boys. "But today we need to finish preparing for the four clients we have coming tomorrow. They're dirt biking and going for a llama-cart ride."

Peter hoped they were experienced, keen dirt bikers.

"I've tuned up the bikes," Jake said, a spoon halfway to his mouth. "Made sure the chains were in good repair and the cables adjusted."

"I know. Very good," Sergei said.

"And I cleared that fallen tree off the upper trail like you asked," Peter spoke up. There were an upper and a lower trail on the ranch, both of which led to the A-frame cabin on a far bluff. The cabin was outfitted with bunk beds and a fireplace. Sergei used it for lunch stops as well as to accommodate clients wanting an overnight trip. Mostly, Peter had figured out, he reserved the more challenging upper trail for the bikes, and the flatter lower trail for the llama carts. In between the two trails was a sheep pasture. There the ever-alert guard llama, Hero, watched over Sergei's flock when they weren't in a smaller pasture near the motocross track.

"Good work," Sergei said, nodding at the two boys. "Today is Sunday, of course, so you have the afternoon free."

"Yup, we're meeting Dana at the pool for some freestyle stunts," Peter reported. He could hardly wait.

"Tsk, tsk," Natalia said as she shook her head before pulling a second loaf of bread from the oven. "Is dangerous and *gloopy*."

"What does *gloopy* mean?" Peter asked. He might as well learn a Russian word or two while he was here.

"It means silly," Sergei responded with a smile. "Going for Saturday's freestyle purse, you and Dana? Just don't hurt my bikes, please. Or yourselves," he added as an afterthought when Natalia wagged a manicured finger at him.

Peter laughed. "We'll play safely," he assured them, ignoring Jake's frown. Jake's disapproval of freestyle tricks merely amused him. And Jake's obsession with "wrenching," or tinkering with bikes, bored him. Peter loved action and risk. He loved the bolt of adrenalin that zooming bikes into the sky provided. He thrived on the challenge of landing a trick, the excitement of learning new moves. He couldn't understand how a guy would prefer to hang out in the race pits, hands greasy, ear to a motor. Sure the sport needed mechanics. Great racers couldn't be great without great mechanics. But Peter couldn't fathom preferring wrenches to handlebars in your hands. And he figured that if Jake would just get out there and straddle a machine more often, he'd totally understand the appeal of freestyle.

Peter savored every crumb of Natalia's bread and every last drop of the stew's rich flavor. He enjoyed the warm embrace of the kitchen, wished he and Jake could eat all their meals here. But they were lowly helpers, lucky to be invited in at all, he reminded himself as Natalia rose and moved to the sink.

Nice that Sergei didn't really mind the boys and Dana messing around with the ranch's bikes, even attempting tricks over the pool. Of course, Sergei himself had probably destroyed more bikes in his time than the boys would ever ride. And he'd undoubtedly broken a few bones along the way. Peter could imagine Natalia perfecting her tsk-tsking over the several years they'd been married. They'd only just turned thirty, and here they were on the other side of the world from where they'd grown up, working a ranch and finding occasional time to be playful on the side.

"Why did you decide to come to the US?" Peter asked, glancing at the glitter polish on Natalia's toenails.

Sergei smiled, stood, and snuck an arm around his wife's bare shoulders. Natalia pecked his cheek before turning her warm smile on Peter.

"America is land of dreams," she said, gesturing around the ranch-house kitchen and out the window, as if that explained everything. "So much room, so much possibility."

"I may not be an official veterinarian here yet," Sergei added, "but I have animals to care for, a ranch, and a motocross track. And my bikes purr like healthy cats." He grinned, withdrew his arm from Natalia to cross his muscular biceps over his chest, then studied the floor as his smile faded a little. "And soon, I will be a vet again," he added determinedly.

"You bet you will!" Peter said, reaching for some more of Natalia's bread. He could get used to hanging out at Back-of-Beyond Ranch; he'd decided that Sergei and Natalia were good folks.

"Well, time for me to saddle up a horse and go check on Hero and his sheep," Sergei said. "Funny American name for a llama, Hero," he mused, shaking his head.

"When we can afford a new baby llama, we give it Russian name," Natalia suggested. She rose to wrap a loaf of bread in paper and push it on Peter.

"Please, for Dana," she said. "You will deliver it to her?" Her blue eyes were pleading like it was a big deal. So Peter shrugged, smiled, and accepted it.

"I'll come watch you and Dana biking later," Jake said as they parted at the doorway. "Be careful."

"Okay," Peter replied, knowing Jake preferred the tool corner of the barn. He wandered back behind the ranch house. A quick check of the pool revealed no sign of Dana, so he turned his boots toward her little trailer nearby.

"Dana?" he asked as he drew near the door. No reply.

"Dana?" he repeated, lifting his hand to pull on the door, which was ajar.

There was no one inside. He climbed the two steps and decided to drop the bread on the tiny fold-down linoleum table. Her trailer made his and Jake's seem big, he thought ruefully as his eyes did a quick perusal of her quarters. Books on llamas and motocross racing lined a sagging bookshelf over her unmade bed. Clothes were strewn about the worn upholstery of the kitchen-nook seat. Motocross boots sat toppled over in front of a closet hardly big enough for a broom.

He lifted the loaf of bread to the table. That's when he drew in his breath. Several syringes sat there: the kind doctors use for giving shots. *Doctors and drug addicts*, Peter thought. As his heart skipped a beat, he diverted the bread loaf to the counter and dropped it there. Hopefully Dana would think Natalia had dropped it off. He nearly tripped in his rush to back up toward the doorway. Then he spun, ran down the steps, and kept running.

"Is that why Dana's so quiet?" his mind demanded. "Do Sergei and Natalia know? What kind of drugs is she into? No, don't even think about it. Maybe there's an explanation. Don't think about it until you have a chance to ask Jake if he knows anything."

Searching for a distraction to halt a flow of other questions he didn't want to ponder, he let his eyes scan the dusty road, the llama paddock, the three-sided llama pen, and the nearby barn. Three pairs of large eyes turned to watch him as the llamas pricked up their long ears and directed their funny "mmmm" sound his way.

He paused and looked at them. Strange to think that the ranch's llamas, unlike horses, could handle the same steep, rutted terrain as the off-road motor-cycles. That's because llamas have two-toed feet, like camels. He moved on, trying to force his mind to stay thinking about llamas, instead of what he'd seen in Dana's trailer. Sergei claimed that llamas were sure-footed on almost anything: sand, snow, even steep hillsides. They could handle pretty much everything, Sergei had said, except mud. But it was so dry here on the Washington–Idaho border that mud was a rare thing. And that's good, because according to Sergei, llamas are like donkeys the way they hate rain. Guess there's not that much rain in the Peruvian Andes of South America where llamas mostly come from.

Only when he reached the pool and heard the chainsaw-like *vrooom* of Dana's bike accelerating up the wooden ramp did he breathe freely. He hoped she'd have no way of knowing what he'd seen in her trailer. And that she wasn't doing freestyle tricks while under the influence of drugs.

4   Freestyle Tricks

From the barn, Jake could hear the high-pitched screams of Peter's and Dana's dirt-bike engines. He tuned his ears into Dana's in particular, having worked on its carburetor earlier that morning. As he stowed away his tools on Sergei's massive tool bench, he smiled, pleased with the sound.

She'd seemed happy with the repair job, too, not that she'd said much. She never said much. You had to kind of read her by the way she shrugged or turned her face or nodded while studying the floor of the barn. She was like a motorcycle: she communicated less with words than with motions, which one could learn to decode with time and patience. Maybe that's how she read her llamas, Jake mused as he tossed an oily rag into a bucket. Peter would howl with laughter at that notion, but Peter was a man of action and an endless stream of words. Jake was a quiet, patient mechanic.

"Guess I'd better go watch those two," he addressed Scout, the ranch's dog, who had entered the barn to escape the heat. "Though it'll only encourage Peter."

As he stepped around the barn's corner, he sucked in his breath and stood stock-still. Straight ahead, Peter was upside down thirty-five feet in the air over the pool. As Jake continued to watch, boy and bike drew a neat loop in the air, as if riding a roller coaster on an invisible track. Standing on his foot pegs with front tire slightly drawn up, Peter and his steed plunged neatly into the pool's blocks of foam. There, they imprinted and bounced back softly, like Natalia's finger testing the top of a springy cake just out of the oven.

Jake couldn't stop a surge of pride for his friend, any more than he could stop his head from shaking. He'd never seen Peter do a backflip, and he wasn't sure he wanted to see it again, at least not anywhere but over a pool. How many times could a guy do a backflip before something went wrong? Freestyle was a lottery. Way more than motocross racing, it was high-stakes gambling. It required nerves of steel, but also a willingness to do hospital time, maybe even spend the rest of your life in a wheelchair. Was the risk in perfecting a backflip worth a $100 purse at a small-time race intermission? No way. But Jake knew better than to try and tell Peter what to do. So he might as well appreciate the perfection of that stunt.

"Peter!" he called out as Peter used a small hand crane stationed at the side of the pool to lift his bike out of it. But the roar of Dana's 125 drowned out his congratulations. He turned in time to see it rocket up the curved wooden ramp and sail into the air as casually as an airplane. There, it lingered as if sensing that the clear blue sky needed a shiny ornament. As it went into a slow-motion arc, Dana whipped it—put the bike's spokes nearly parallel to the ground for a split second—then lifted her right leg off its peg and pulled it all the way over the seat to the other side of the bike, as if about to dismount mid-air. Hands still gripping the handlebars, she extended that same leg all the way back, head and body following it for extra effect, like a gymnast attempting the splits. Then, just as casually, she swung her right leg back over the saddle and hit the pool's padding while standing, feet on her pegs and well braced.

A Nac-Nac, Jake remembered: a trick made famous by motocross legend Jeremy McGrath. Peter had told him that move was tougher than it looked. Good for her. He wondered if it was fun hitting the foam, like leaping into a giant pile of leaves or falling into a stack of pillows. He was tempted to jump into this strange pool sometime when there was no danger of motorcycles falling on him. But he had no interest in landing a motorcycle in there himself. These two could play all they wanted, but even soft foam could bend a brake or clutch lever, or make the throttle get stuck. He'd be busy checking over both their bikes later. Lucky for them he was so dedicated, he mused with a half smile. Especially Peter, who was clueless and lazy about anything mechanical.

Sure, Peter could ride well. Way better than Jake. But Jake took pride in knowing that he'd saved Peter from roaring onto a track with mechanical difficulties more than once. Peter couldn't seem to get how important a well tuned machine was, and how taking a little more time to learn about his bike's workings would give him an edge. Not that Jake was going to change his buddy. So Peter should figure out he wasn't going to change Jake, who not-so-secretly dreamed of being one of the star mechanics that pro racers want.

"Hey, Dana," he heard Peter call to his fellow freestyler. "Can you do a Double Can-Can or a Lazy-Boy?"

Dana, working the crane to pull her 200-pound bike out of the pool, paused to shake her head no.

"A Double Can-Can isn't that much harder than a Nac-Nac," Peter urged her. "BMXers do it all the time."

Like she wouldn't know that, Jake thought. He could tell from the set of the girl's shoulders that she wasn't going to try it today, whatever Peter said. Jake was just as sure that Peter was going to do both those tricks right now, in front of her, to let her know who was boss. Good old Peter, predictable as a rooster strutting past the henhouse.

Jake saw Dana's head turn his way as Peter leapt on his bike and swung around to line up for the ramp. He recalled his conversation with Peter earlier:

"Needles? Think she's a druggie?"

"Hope not. Doesn't look like that kind."

"But what would that stuff be for otherwise?"

"Dunno. Think we should tell Sergei?"

"No way. Not till we see her shooting up, or she looks strung out."

"Okay, we'll just keep an eye on her."

Jake strolled toward Dana, eyes on her bike to make sure it had survived the pool landing fine.

"It's good," she said, aligning the handlebars with the forks as if reading his mind.

Jake nodded soberly and turned to make sure he'd have a good view of Peter's next aerial show.

"You don't do freestyle?" she asked. As always, she wouldn't look at him while speaking. He followed her eyes to the sky, saw a large bald eagle coasting in circles on air currents high above.

"Nope," Jake said. Slyly, to test her, he explained, "Peter is Jeremy. I'm Skip."

He was pleased when a smile tugged at her lips. "You mean Skip Norfolk, Jeremy McGrath's mechanic."

So she knew of the legendary wrencher for one of the greatest motocross racers ever. Jake nodded, eyes on the ramp as it reverberated under Peter's acceleration.

"So you want to be a big-time factory mechanic."

Jake nodded again, smiling.

He watched her pull her eyes from the eagle as Peter's bike shot into the air. At the peak of the jump, Peter used his considerable upper-body strength to lift his entire body off the bike and kick both feet first to one side, then the other.

"Like a cheerleader shaking pompoms," Jake said loud enough to be heard over Peter's motor, smiling at his own humor. But as he watched, he saw one of Peter's hands slip a little on the bike grip, causing one hip to hit the seat before he had a chance to separate his feet and re-straddle the bike. He was going to hit the pool while sitting sidesaddle.

"Uh-oh," Jake muttered as the front wheel sank into the foam. The bike bounced and bucked off its rider, then cartwheeled and hit the pool's wall. There, it scraped a graffiti-style mark on the already peeling paint. Peter landed beside the bike, sinking into the foam like a dud tennis ball. He lay still for a moment, as if contemplating the cloudless bowl of blue above. Then he sprang up with a sheepish smile and bent over the bike. Jake groaned to see a dent in the gas tank.

"Practise makes perfect," Peter called. "Just a little dent," he added. "Good thing we have a mechanic in the house."

Jake glanced at Dana. Her eyes were once again fastened on the eagle, whose circles—without help from wing movement—were becoming a slowly downward spiral.

"Peter can't even change his own air filter," Jake found himself saying to her as he moved forward to make sure his buddy was okay. But when he turned to see Dana's response to that, he was surprised to see that she'd leapt off her bike and was sprinting toward the llama shed as if it was on fire or something. Out of the corner of his eye, he saw Sergei running from the opposite direction, also toward the shed, which was just out of view from the pool.

"What's up?" Peter shouted.

"Let's find out," Jake replied, offering his hand to help Peter out of the pool.

Leaving the bikes, they began to run.

Jake witnessed the eagle's final drop into the llama enclosure and saw its talons snatch a panicked white hen. Only when it had the hen between its claws did its wings begin to flap, fighting gravity to lift its prey. As the helpless hen emitted ear-splitting squawks and panicked flapping, white feathers floated down on a melee of crazed hens running in circles below their mate's thrashing feet. Sergei was shouting and bending to the ground for a rock to throw. Dana, to Jake's puzzlement, had slipped into the enclosure, unfastened a gate, and backed up against a fence post, calmly calling the llamas by name. All three llamas had run up the field to get closer to the action, ears flattened in excitement. Furball began hissing.

As Sergei's rock missile missed its target, Rocky the Rooster flew at the eagle, which, despite being several times the size of the hen in its grip, had not yet lifted itself out of the rooster's range. Rocky's sharp spurs raked the eagle's breast feathers, a show of bravery Jake figured should earn him a soldier's medal.

"Go Rocky go!" Peter was shouting, as if it was a sports match.

Jake was astounded by Rocky's nerve. It was like a house cat picking a fight with a mountain lion. With one good blow, the eagle's beak could have split the rooster's small skull in two and poked out the other side like a sword. None of the humans present were about to approach the giant predator. Its wingspan was wider than Jake was tall. Its talons were the size of the hooks in the barn designed to pick up hay bales. Newborn lambs had been known to be carried away by eagles when not under the protection of sheepdogs or guard llamas. Rocky, Jake decided, wasn't about to save that hen without trading his own life for it.

Rocky's attack and the threat of Sergei's stones seemed to enrage the eagle, now three feet off the ground. Maintaining its lock-grip on the struggling hen, it turned its sharp beak and beating wings at its attacker. Rocky fearlessly did the same.

For several noisy seconds, the two birds battled. Sergei's arm was lifted but frozen; Jake could see he dared not risk hitting the rooster or hen. Finally the eagle dropped the hen and closed its talons over Rocky, lifting him high over the dusty enclosure.

By now, Furball had charged into the enclosure. He raised his behind and kicked at the air several feet below the rising rooster, emitting a sound somewhere between a whinny and a screech. Too late, Jake thought. If Furball intended to karate-chop the eagle, he was out of luck. The giant bird of prey had finally risen out of range of a llama hoof.

Fastening his eyes on Furball, Jake watched as the young llama they called "the devil" flattened his ears as far back as they'd go, cocked his head, and stretched his long neck upward. He opened his mouth wide, curled his camel-like lips, and blew the biggest spit wad Jake had ever seen—directly at the eagle's face.

Bull's eye. A firehose volume of composted green guck struck the eagle right between the eyes. It looked like smelly, half-digested alfalfa sprouts, and, even several feet below it, Jake had to plug his nose. Totally, totally gross. The eagle's reaction was swift. Its talons retracted, the rooster dropped from the sky, and the eagle flew away. Rocky hit the dust at Dana's feet and lay motionless. The hen it had saved clucked noisily and raised clouds of dust running toward the other hens.

Before Dana could stoop to inspect Rocky, Sergei had dashed to its aid. He lifted it gently and carried its limp body to a straw bale in the chicken coop.

"Good boy, Furball," he said as he passed the llama, in a voice that reflected amazement at what had just gone down. "And thanks, Dana."

All she had done was unlatch the gate, but clearly she had counted on the llama doing something heroic. Jake half expected Dana to wrap congratulatory arms around Furball. Instead, she just nodded at her boss, turned toward Furball, and lifted a carrot from a shelf in the llama shelter. With a gentle flow of words, she proceeded to coax Furball to turn around and head back through the gate, into the field where his mates stood. Furball followed his guide, happily chomping his carrot as his woolly sides brushed the gateposts.

When Peter walked over as if to pat Furball's rump before it disappeared through the gate, Dana turned and said in a commanding voice Jake had no idea she owned, "Stay back, Peter, unless you want to be part of a freestyle move that doesn't involve a dirt bike."

5   The Llamas

"**Y**ou knew he was going to do that? You knew he could spit that far if he didn't make it in time to kick that crazy eagle?" Peter asked Dana, standing back as his eyes moved from llama handler to llamas. "Is the hen hurt? Do you think Rocky'll be okay? Did you know it'd be Furball and not the other two llamas who'd come to the rescue? And how come?"

He gestured to Salt and Pepper, Furball's larger and, according to Sergei, calmer companions. Peter liked Pepper best; the long-necked black animal seemed the most playful out in the field. He was always sticking his nose into things, and he'd be the first to come galloping—if what llamas do is called galloping—when a visitor arrived at the ranch.

Dana barely glanced at Peter, then shrugged. The girl drove him crazy. He'd asked her perfectly reasonable questions, and she couldn't even be bothered to answer.

"The hen's fine except for being frantic. Not sure there's much I can do for Rocky," Sergei finally ruled as he emerged from the henhouse. "I don't think he has any broken bones, but he's stunned. He'll pull himself together by morning. I'm going to ask you not to tease him like you've been doing, Peter," the vet added soberly, "when he does revive."

Peter hung his head a little and nodded.

"I'll make sure he doesn't," Jake offered, squinting his eyes at his trailer mate in mock sternness.

"Good thinking, Dana," Sergei said. "You sure know those animals. It worked, anyway."

The boys turned their heads to Dana. She avoided their eyes but nodded ever so briefly at Sergei.

"I have to tell Natalia what happened." With that, Sergei turned and ambled toward the ranch house.

Peter watched Dana fill a battered metal bucket with water from a faucet and pour its contents into the water trough in the llama shed. "Freshening up their water for them? Guess Furball has to be thirsty after losing that lot," he commented, determined to get this anti-social girl to answer him. It was just plain rude the way she almost always looked the other way and hardly ever said anything. Maybe Sergei was right about how she spent so much time with animals that she sometimes forgot she was a human being.

He watched her finish emptying her bucket and move back a little as Furball wandered into the shed to lower his head into the trough. She stood there—watchful, not like she was afraid of him. More as if she knew he wanted space.

"Yes," Dana responded, startling Peter for a second. She turned and eyed Peter briefly, as if measuring his real level of interest. "Yes, I'm freshening up their water. Llamas are like camels. They're related to camels, you know. When they eat, their food goes through three stomachs before it's digested."

"They have three stomachs?" Peter asked dumbly. "I guess if they're like camels, they don't need much water, either."

"What do they eat?" Jake asked.

"Grains," she replied, "and sometimes fruit or carrots." She opened a cupboard in the shed, took out a former cookie tin, and pulled off its lid. She lifted a small metal scoop from inside it. "Want to feed Salt or Pepper a snack?"

"You bet!" Peter enthused, as Jake replied, "Yes!"

Dana poured what looked like birdseed into their outstretched hands. But she waited to unlatch the gate until Furball had finished drinking and moved out of the shed into the field.

"Salt, Pepper!" she called.

The two large llamas came trotting over, ears up, their large, almond-shaped eyes on the boys. Peter liked how they knew their names. And he liked how they kind of swayed when they walked. Their legs seemed so spindly beneath those thick coats of coarse hair. Their front legs were slightly shorter than their back legs, reminding him of a jacked-up car. From the back, they looked like sheep on over-tall legs, but their necks were definitely like camels'. Their cute faces were goat-like, except for not having little beards on their chins, and the long ears were nearly like donkeys' ears. They chewed their cuds like a goat, faces working back and forth. Their long eyelashes were unlike any other creature's Peter had seen. And then there were those two-toed camel-type feet with a soft pad beneath. That made their tracks in the dirt like an elk's or a deer's. Just plain weird. Llamas were like the kind of animal a confused child might draw.

Peter broke into a grin when Pepper sauntered straight up to him. Salt had chosen Jake.

"Pepper likes you 'cause you're wearing a black T-shirt," Dana said. "He's attracted to anything black. He totally ignores our white lambs and goats but takes a big interest in the black ones."

"That's cool," Peter said. He held out his cupped hands. Pepper eyed the handful of grain but first raised his muzzle to Peter's nose and breathed out.

The breath was soft and sweet.

"He's greeting you. Breathe back on him through your nose," Dana instructed Peter. "That's the way llamas greet one another."

Peter exhaled through his nose in a return greeting. This prompted Pepper to nod and flick his tail. After one more nose-to-nose session, Pepper plunged his muzzle into the grain. Peter's heart warmed to the creature. The llama's nose was soft as velvet, like a rabbit's or a puppy's. Its softness pushed about in his hands. There was no show of teeth; the lips seemed to work like the hose of a silent vacuum cleaner. But Peter was surprised how big Pepper was close up; you wouldn't want him to accidentally step on your toes. Peter was glad he was wearing motocross boots.

"These guys are as big as ponies," Peter observed, resisting the temptation to run a hand down Pepper's dark neck. "Can you ride them?"

"Small children can," Dana said, forking some hay into a rack.

"Wouldn't it be fun to have one of these as a pet?" Pepper was finished his grain and had raised his head, looking toward the shed to see if Dana might refill Peter's hands.

"Not one llama. You'd have to have two," Dana scolded Peter as if he'd said something seriously bad.

"Huh?"

"Llamas are herd animals. If you raise one without a companion, it goes berserk."

"Berserk?" Peter and Jake asked together.

Dana had turned her head to watch Furball, who'd wandered over to a tree to inspect its just-out-of-reach branches.

"Furball is what they call a berserk llama," Dana said, sadness in her voice. "He's unpredictable around humans because he was an un-neutered male raised alone, against the advice of the llama farm that sold him. Most berserk llamas end up having to be destroyed."

"Destroyed?" Peter was alarmed. He looked at Furball. "Sergei isn't going to kill Furball, is he? Furball just saved Rocky the Rooster," he added, looking toward the henhouse.

"I'm working with Furball to make him more cooperative," Dana said. "Sergei takes in berserk llamas because he knows that I know how to work with them."

"Like how?" Peter asked, picturing Dana giving Furball "time outs" in the corner of the field when he misbehaved.

"The llama carts. I run him on the trails out to the cabin on the point and back every day in harness between Salt and Pepper. He's learning from them. He's starting to fit in and calm down."

Peter rubbed his neck. "Like sled dogs," he remarked. "I've read that's how they train new huskies: they put them in between experienced ones. Cool. Can I ride in the llama cart sometime?"

Dana formed a half smile. "Sometime. But Sergei says we have clients tomorrow. So you'd better get back to the pool and fix your dirt bike."

"Oh yeah," Peter said, glancing back toward the pool, where it seemed like hours since they'd practised their freestyle tricks. "Jake, got your tool box ready? I have a patient for you."

He saw Dana start to open her mouth as if she was going to comment on his assigning his bike repairs to Jake. But she wisely held her tongue. Ha, Peter thought. She can't say anything after she had Jake help her with a repair this morning. Anyway, it wasn't any of her business. Peter was useless at repairs. He was all thumbs with tools. He had no patience for that kind of thing, and he didn't need to do it with Jake around. In return, of course, he coached Jake on dirt-bike technique. Too bad Jake got as bored with listening to that as Peter did listening to stuff about bike repair.

"Doctor Jake is on his way to the barn for his tool kit," Jake replied, smiling and squaring his shoulders. "Meet you at the pool."

6   Dirt Trails

Jake sized up the clients from the trailer window as they piled out of their minivan the next morning.

"A mom, a dad, a boy maybe ten years old—he'll need an 80—and a little girl."

"Maybe the mom and girl won't go biking," Peter said as he pulled on his jeans and reached for his boots.

"The boy is running over to the bikes already. The mom and girl are leaning over the fence and calling to the llamas," Jake reported as he dumped the ends of his hot cocoa down the trailer's sink and grabbed his baseball cap from a hook by the door.

"So maybe Dana's got customers for the day, too. Think she actually talks to them while she's steering the llama cart?"

"If they asked a direct question, she'd answer.

Doubt they get much more out of her than that."

"Some guide she is. Guides are supposed to have lots of personality. Like me."

"Yeah, well you and your personality are going to get a lecture from Sergei if you don't finish getting dressed faster. I'm outta here." Jake threw open the door and leapt down its steps. He walked to where Sergei and Natalia were engaging the father in animated conversation. They turned as Jake strolled up.

"And this is Jake, one of our junior guides," Sergei was saying. "He's also an ace mechanic if you need any repairs done on the trail. Jake, this is Cal Hoffman, visiting from Kelowna, Canada, just north of here."

"Nice to meet you," Jake said, extending his hand to the big-framed man. He noticed the man's black T-shirt advertised a heavy-metal band, and his arms sported what Jake figured was the world's biggest collection of tattoos.

Cal grunted in a not-unfriendly manner and jerked his head toward his wife. "Like we arranged, my wife and daughter want only the llama-cart ride. Eddie over there can't wait to get set up on the dirt bikes. Hope the trail's not easy. My son likes a challenge."

Jake had a feeling that meant he and Peter would need to keep a close eye on the kid. Minutes later, as he reached for his fanny-belt tool kit from the garage, he decided to toss in an inner tube and some filter oil.

Sergei had given Jake, Peter, and Dana identical black soft-leather fanny belts. All four, including Sergei's, hung from marked pegs in the barn. Jake's bulged with his crescent wrench, pliers, multi-bit screwdriver, tire irons, tube of lubricant, patch kit, electrical tape, small flashlight, and first-aid items. It was definitely filled to capacity. Peter's, on the other hand, bulged mostly with granola bars, although Sergei had insisted that Peter stuff in a multi-tool, flashlight, duct tape, and first aid pouch, too. Dana's pack looked as full as Jake's, although with what, Jake didn't know. Her belt held a curiously rectangular object at one end, something resembling a calculator. Repair stuff for the llama-cart wheels, maybe?

"We should mark our bags. They all look alike," Peter said from behind Jake as both boys reached for theirs.

"They don't look one bit alike the way they're packed," Jake replied as they strapped on their fanny packs and exited the barn, headed for the bikes. "Although they might if you'd bother to bring your own tools."

"Hey, someone has to bring replacement calories," Peter teased back. "There might even be snacks in here for my wrencher if he's nice to me."

Within half an hour, their party of five—Sergei, Jake, Peter, Cal, and Eddie—were roaring up the forested upper trail, waving goodbye to Dana and her female clients seated on the narrow seat of the cart behind the llamas. The llama team was headed along the lower trail.

"See you at the cabin for lunch!" Sergei shouted. "May the best team win!"

Sergei led, with Eddie's front fender immediately behind his rear tire as if the boy resented having a guide. Eddie's dad was followed by Jake and Peter, who motored up the trail behind. The boys exchanged amused looks when Eddie, to show off, popped a wheelie.

Jake was more impressed when Eddie mimicked Sergei's leap over a small log. Like his guide, the kid chose the lowest point to cross. He lofted his front tire over with his body carefully centered and his chest and head right over the handlebars, then eased the rear wheel across at low speed. His father did the same, much faster and more confidently.

Jake was about to go for it when he heard Peter's voice behind him. "It's all about timing, old buddy. You wheelie it only if you're good and need to do it fast."

Annoyed that Peter would think he needed advice for jumping a log, Jake paused, only to have Peter zoom past him. Jake watched Peter ride toward the log at low speed, then lift his front wheel up before it touched the log, like a rearing horse. As his frame came down on the top of the log, Jake expected to see Peter's rear wheel kicking up as its rear suspension rebounded. That would send him over the bars, which would serve him right for acting as if Jake didn't know what he was doing. But the bike eased down and over the log; his buddy had exhibited the perfect control of a veteran log-jumper.

Jake sped up and duplicated Peter's moves. So what if his landing was a little shaky? He might not be as good a rider as Peter, but he didn't need Peter to tell him how to jump a log. They were both guides, after all! Peter was being bossy just to make up for secretly feeling dumb about being useless when it came to mechanics, Jake reasoned.

"Hey, Jake and Peter. Watch me!" Eddie's boyish voice called out.

They looked ahead in time to see first Eddie, then Sergei, twist their handlebars with just the right timing to ride between two trees.

"Kid's not bad," Jake said to Peter as the boys followed suit.

Although Sergei had set a conservative pace, it didn't take him long to tire of Eddie gunning up beside him every few minutes and asking to go faster. Soon, the entire procession was playing high-speed slalom with trees and boulders, whipping around bends, roaring up stony gullies, and splashing through shallow creeks.

"Watch out for tree roots and sharp rocks hidden under leaves or moss," Sergei instructed once, when they'd pulled up all in a row and idled to catch their breath before entering more forest. "And for branches that can take your head off when you're going between trees."

"What about water crossings?" Eddie asked.

That made Jake smile. He'd been reading up on how to prepare the bikes for water crossings. With Sergei's permission, he'd sealed the electrical systems to keep the engines from quitting after a dousing, smeared the engine joints with silicone, and covered the air-box holes with duct tape. He was pretty confident he'd done a good job.

"You choose the shortest and shallowest place to cross," Sergei advised, leaning back in his seat and lifting his helmet off so everyone could hear him.

"Yeah," Peter interrupted, as if determined to play guide. "You stand up so you can use your knees to help you with a sudden dip or rise. And don't splash so much that it gets into your air filter."

"And walk your bike if there's sharp rocks or you'll get a flat," Cal added.

Jake wasn't listening by then. He'd turned his

eyes and ears to Peter's bike, which even on idle was spluttering.

"Hey Peter, cut your motor and let me have a look at your bike," Jake said.

"It's fine," Peter said, lifting his feet to his foot pegs. He looked as if he was about to gun it to peel back onto the trail.

"Peter!" Sergei shouted, startling all four team members. "When Jake says cut it, cut it."

Peter killed his motor, shrugged, and dismounted.

Jake walked over and bent down beside the 125's tank. He unscrewed the gas cap, saw the dark gold liquid sparkle at him from near the top of the tank. No need to flip the valve under the tank to activate the reserve tank. He scratched his head, then squinted at Peter and frowned.

"You did get Sergei to teach you to clean your air filter yesterday like we agreed, right? Since you wouldn't let me teach you?"

"Nah, didn't have time. I'll do it later today," Peter replied without looking up.

Jake frowned. He shook his head, popped open the side cover, and examined the spongy filter. It was covered in mud and debris.

"Filthy," he muttered. "No wonder it's bogging on you. Your bike's going to be running like a toad— jerking and jumping—by the end of this trip. Man, are you lazy! I'll shake the worst of it out for now in case it helps. Watch me do it so you'll know how."

"It's fine. Stop worrying."

Jake looked up, saw Peter sit on a nearby tree stump to unzip his fanny pack. Looking for food, no doubt.

"Peter," Jake said with annoyance. "Just watch me for a second in case you need to know."

"Sure, whatever it takes so we can get back on the trail," Peter suggested, chewing on a granola bar and glancing over.

"Peter," Sergei said. "Listen carefully in case you need to know something when Jake isn't around. Your lack of interest in how your machine runs is going to get you in trouble someday." His tone was friendly, even teasing, but Jake noticed that Peter stopped eating.

"No problem," Peter replied, rising and moving to stand near Jake. "But Jake and I are a team: he's my wrencher and I'm his moto-coach. Not that he listens to any of my technique advice any more than I listen to his techie talk," he added, grin widening.

This prompted Sergei to chuckle, then look thoughtful, as if he was preparing a retort.

Jake, ignoring Peter's last comment, had the air filter out of its air box and was extracting a bit of gasoline to pour over it. Eddie came and plunked down on the ground beside him, raising a cloud of dust that made Jake cough. Cal followed him over and peered at Jake. At length, Peter rose and wandered over, his chewing noises annoying Jake.

Once the gasoline had removed the dirty gray of the filter, Jake poured water from his water bottle over the filter, then wrung it out carefully and massaged in foam filter oil.

"It's sticky like syrup," he informed Peter as Eddie drew closer to watch. "Catches any of the dirt from getting into the motor." Finally, he popped it back in its box.

Sergei ambled over to pause between his junior guides. First, he leaned over to inspect Jake's work, then rested one arm on Jake's shoulder and the other on Peter's. "Good work, Jake, and good watching, Peter. But your system is going to break down at some point unless you two are joined at the hip. I'm a vet, so I know it's not good enough to know an animal's biology. I have to know something about its behavior, too. What it wants, who it is. The two are connected. Like you North Americans say, 'body and soul.' I can't fix one without knowing something about the other."

"Body and soul," Peter mused aloud, plopping back down on his stump. "Sounds like a hair salon where my mom would go. Are you saying motorcycles have souls, Sergei?" His face was posed for ridicule.

Sergei's bushy eyebrows knit themselves together. "Peter, if you want to pull off a special move on a motorcycle, you have to know every inch of what it can do. That means understanding it inside and out. If you know its mechanics, you also know it has a soul."

Peter turned his smile into a frown but said nothing.

"Your dirt bike has to know how badly you want something before it'll help you pull it off. It's okay to talk to your machine, you know. Just like Dana talks to the llamas."

Jake watched Peter wrinkle his nose and glance around, as if checking out whether anyone was taking Sergei seriously. No one spoke or moved. Eddie's wide eyes moved from Sergei to Peter.

"Well, you've got a point, boss," Peter allowed. "I need to pay more attention to mechanical stuff, and Jake needs to take riding more seriously. I keep telling Jake that the factory mechanics do test-rides way more than he does. I think he should try out some freestyle, too."

"Give it up, Peter," Jake growled.

"No really, Jake. Think of Alley Seymar. An ex-pro racer who became a famous mechanic for Kevin Windham. He knew his stuff *on* the bike before he went for full-time in the pits. That's the kind of wrencher that racers want."

Jake raised his head, rolled his eyes, then bent back to adjusting Peter's seat.

"True, Peter," Sergei interjected, "but even a great mechanic is helped or hurt by how well his racer can explain what seems to be going wrong on the track. The best racer-wrencher duos have learned to communicate. They've made more effort than either of you to learn from each other. But enough said."

Enough said for sure, Jake thought darkly as silence held for a few seconds. Maybe Sergei and Peter had valid points, but mostly Jake was feeling annoyed with Peter's test-ride comment in front of the clients. He also knew it wouldn't be professional to let it show.

"Do you always use gasoline to clean your air filter?" Eddie asked.

"You betcha, kid! Though you can use a solvent, too. You're smart," Jake said, patting Eddie on the head. Eddie squirmed but smiled. Jake clapped dust off his hands, and stowed his tools carefully in his fanny belt before zipping it shut.

They hit the trail again, roaring one at a time up and down the ever-changing terrain. Eddie's dad looked totally comfortable on his machine, except where the trail grew narrow.

Jake watched as Eddie dodged boulders close enough to rub the green of their moss onto his knee-pads and sped up over bumps to catch air. The boy leaned in all the right places and dashed between tree trunks no farther apart than the width of his handle-bars. So far, he was "destroying" the trail.

There were boulders and logs to dodge or jump, and rocky-bottomed creeks to cross. Good thing it didn't rain much around these parts, or some of the sections would be totally sketchy. He glanced at the edge of the trails, where passing bikes had obviously chewed up the terrain a bit. Motorcycles were always making new ruts and holes on a dirt track; there was no escaping the fact. That's why environmental-ists were always trying to shut down dirt-bike areas. Trouble is, thanks to expanding suburbs and environ-mentalists, politicians were way more into shutting down trails than helping maintain some, or designat-ing new ones. That just forced dirt bikers into ever more concentrated regions, including watersheds. At least here, the trails had been designated and were being maintained regularly by both Sergei and the Forest Service, limiting environmental impact.

Jake winced once as Eddie veered off the trail to run his bike through a rare muddy patch. So much for having cleaned that bike's sprockets, he thought. Guess the kid doesn't know that mud can wear them down fast. Then again, that's what dirt bikes are made for, and anyway, why would the kid care on a rental bike and guided tour?

As the group emerged from the woods to a clearing above his sheep field, Sergei signaled them over. "Refueling stop," he said, cutting his motor and swinging a leg off his bike.

"Refueling?" Eddie asked. Jake calculated they'd been out for close to an hour this morning already. And he knew Eddie would like the refueling station.

"You bet," Sergei replied, setting his helmet on a stump and pointing to a tree at the edge of the clearing.

Eddie watched, wide-eyed, as Sergei strolled to the tree and seemed to magically produce a ladder from under the bushes behind it. Sergei leaned the ladder up against the tree and began to climb. Jake watched the boy lift his eyes until he spotted a platform curtained by army-style camouflage fabric. Jake moved closer as Sergei reached his arms into the camouflaged section and pulled out two five-gallon gas containers.

The group heard some Russian curses, saw the ranch owner's face go puffy with anger. "Those Bateman brats have been stealing gas again. They take so little they think I won't notice. But I can tell, and if I ever get my hands on them ..."

He looked down at the group staring up at him, coughed, and seemed to make an effort to calm his voice. "The next property over is owned by a farmer named Martin Bateman," Sergei snorted. "A farmer whose barn has more stolen car parts than farm animals. He has three wild boys who run their 80s around this trail like it's theirs. They terrorize our lambs, and now they're stealing our gas. If I ever get my hands on those little thieves ..."

Jake and Peter looked at each other. Jake hadn't heard about these neighbors before. And he wasn't sure Sergei should be cursing them out in front of clients. But Sergei was Sergei, and when he was rankled, the world knew about it.

After a few more Russian curses, the big man seemed to settle down. He looped a nearby rope through the handles of the gas containers and lowered them to Jake's and Peter's waiting hands.

"Cool treehouse. Can I climb up there?" Eddie asked.

7   Sidehilling

Sergei smiled and shrugged. "It's not a treehouse; it's a refueling station. But sure, you can come up."

Jake opened the gas containers, unscrewed the dirt bikes' gas caps, and topped up all the motorcycles' tanks as the others climbed up the ladder. He recapped the containers, tied them back on the rope, and let Sergei draw them back up to the treehouse platform. Then he clambered up the ladder to join Sergei and Eddie.

"Daddy, look down there! A llama!" Eddie exclaimed.

"That's Hero. He's a guard llama. He looks after the flock of sheep in that field," Sergei informed Eddie. "He's going to teach those Bateman boys a bruising lesson one of these days."

"A guard llama?" Cal asked from below.

"Yup. More and more farmers are using them. They cost less to keep than sheepdogs and they're just as good at watching over a herd. Because they're larger, they scare away predators more effectively than dogs. Even mountain lions."

"Never heard that before!" Cal said with a smile.

"Hey, dirt bikes are being used for unusual stuff, too," Peter inserted. "Cowboys herd cattle with them, and forest rangers patrol with them."

"True," Sergei agreed. "Trappers, miners, even telephone repair people in woodsy regions use them. Lots of jobs out there for you boys when you finish school!"

Jake tried to picture himself as a telephone repairman on a dirt bike. It made him smile. He kneeled on the high tree platform and looked down on the sheep field. He could see Hero's flock of sheep grazing peacefully. Hero, a large, restless brown-and-white llama, was pacing the fence as if trying to get a whiff of the group of humans in the treehouse. Jake raised his head to look beyond the sheep field.

"Hey Eddie, there's your mom and sister," Jake announced, as a llama cart appeared on the distant, twisting lower trail beneath the field.

Eddie stood up and began to wave. "They're going so slowly!" Eddie complained. "That girl should whip those llamas and see how fast they can go!"

Cal laughed. "She can probably make 'em go fast alright, but I seriously doubt that's what your mom wants."

"Your dad is right," Sergei addressed Eddie. "Especially since they've just come through a section of bends between steep bluffs and a drop-off. It's a section where you have to slow down whether you're in a cart or on a bike."

Jake watched the cart disappear around the trail's curve. He remembered dirt biking down there his first day on the ranch—being nervous about the sheer drop beside the trail. His eyes shifted back to Hero, whose ears were twitching in their direction.

"Can we pet the llama? Please, can we pet that llama?" Eddie was asking Sergei, as Sergei helped him start down the platform's ladder.

"No, Hero isn't a llama you can pet, but we can certainly meet him if you want," Sergei replied. Sergei gazed down the steep, bare hillside beneath them. "You have three choices. You can leave your bikes up here, walk them down to the sheep field, or practise sidehilling. It's too steep to motor down to Hero without sidehilling."

"What's sidehilling?" Eddie asked with big eyes. Jake was relieved someone else had asked, since he'd never heard of it.

"Sidehilling is how you travel across the face of a

hill. The slope and gravity want to take you down; it's all about traction. Sidehilling is very tricky and almost impossible in mud. Luckily, it's all dry today," Sergei told them. "Take lots of time to figure out the smoothest line, and then keep your speed very low."

He paused and looked at Eddie. "Eddie, what did I say you keep your speed?"

"Low," Eddie said, scrunching up his nose.

"Then you weight the outside foot peg—that means you lean harder on the outside than inside peg. You look for the best traction, and you use ruts or little terraces if you can. Sitting is usually better than standing for keeping your center of gravity low."

Jake craned his head to study the steep hillside for lines that might qualify as ruts or terraces. It was mostly just a steep hillside, the kind it'd be fun to roll down—without a bike.

"Don't try sharp turns, keep your momentum, and don't accelerate quickly or you'll get bad wheel spin. Go real easy on the throttle," Sergei finished.

"Got it," Eddie reported.

They started down, one by one, Sergei leading. Jake tried to copy how Sergei kept his weight back, all the way to where the seat joined the rear fender. He noted how the rancher held his arms fully extended, although slightly bent. Jake gripped his chassis like a bareback horse rider determined to stay on his horse.

Jake remembered to press harder on the outside than inside foot peg, and he went easy on the throttle, just like Sergei had instructed.

It was fun, nerve-racking, and sketchy. Where the ground went from hard to soft-packed, Jake gave it a little more gas to keep his momentum. When it went back to soft-packed, he maintained the throttle. If he juiced it, his back wheel would spin, sending a jolt of panic up his spine.

He watched Cal brake-slide the rear end of his motorcycle to establish the direction he wanted to go, then roll on the throttle till he was pointed the right way. He watched Eddie shudder and wheel-spin once or twice, but it wasn't till the boy was halfway down the hill that his 80 started to slide. Jake held his breath as he watched Eddie slide off his bike into the side of the hill. Jake blew a sigh of relief. If Eddie had jumped or fallen the other way, he'd have had a heavy motorcycle falling on top of him, and maybe rolling with him all the way down to where Hero waited by the fence. Hero was now watching them in his calm, perhaps amused way.

"Good stuff, Eddie," Jake called out. The kid had good instincts.

As they approached the bottom, Jake began to apply his rear brakes. That made his engine stall. Panicked, he squeezed the front brake too hard with his right hand. It was the worst thing he could do, of course. The last portion of the steep hillside suddenly seemed to rise and swallow his helmeted head as he did an impromptu end-over-end.

"Ouch!" He lay in the dirt against the fence, wind knocked out of him. He did a mental check for broken bones as his bike lay beside him. He wiggled his toes in his motocross boots. He wiggled his fingers in his gloves. He tensed his arms, legs, and torso. He seemed to be in full working order.

"Jake, old buddy, are you all right?" Peter was running over to him, followed by the pad of other boots.

"I'm fine," Jake replied as he lifted his helmet off and raised his head to inspect his bike. That's when he felt a soft, warm moistness on the back of his neck.

He swiveled his head. "Oh! It's you, Hero!" Hero had poked his head over the wire fence and was breathing on him, as if checking he was okay. Jake remembered to lift his nose slowly to Hero's face and exchange exhales in greeting.

"Mmmm," Hero vocalized from his long throat.

"Mmmm yourself, Hero," Jake said, turning to stand up his motorcycle with Peter's help. Jake bent and inspected the handlebars' alignment with the forks. Then he took a cursory look at the chain.

Sergei was at his side within seconds. "That was quite a spill, Jake. Good thing it was at the bottom and not the top of the hill. You're not injured? Guess you won't brake like that again. Lucky it's soft dirt down here." He grinned at Hero. "I see my assistant has checked you over already."

Hero flicked his ears back and tolerated Sergei's hand resting briefly on his neck. "How's the bike?" Sergei squatted down beside it and began checking for any damage. Cal, Peter, and Eddie crowded around.

"You okay, Jake?" Eddie's worried eyes were scanning Jake's face.

"Yup, it's just the bike I'm worried about."

Sergei's hands were gliding over the bike's vital areas like those of a surgeon: tapping to check for anything loose and touching the connections one by one. "Nah, she's good. No wounds, no breaks, no ruptures, no trauma. She'll purr in a minute," Sergei ruled. "That's your local vet speaking," he added, grinning mischievously and patting the motorcycle in long strokes on its seat, as if it were a large cat.

Jake smiled despite himself. It made sense that a vet who wasn't allowed to practise his profession would transfer his skills and language to his second love, motorcycles.

"Mmmm," Hero intoned.

"I can't believe Hero just sat there as the noise of all these motors came down at him," Cal spoke up.

"Yeah, llamas hardly spook at anything," Sergei said. "If I'm driving a tractor across the field, sometimes I have to stop, get off, and move them out of the way. Motors don't bother them."

The group turned toward Hero, but he obstinately pulled his head back when anyone but Sergei or Jake leaned toward him.

"Hey, how come he likes Jake and Sergei but not me?" Eddie asked, hands on his hips.

Sergei chuckled. "Hero has met Jake three times now, always when I've been with him, so he has figured out that Jake is my friend. That means he has adopted Jake as part of his herd, so to speak."

"Yeah, well he's not okay with me today, and he has met me just as often, always when I'm with you," Peter retorted, voice sounding hurt.

Sergei nodded and looked Peter up and down. "Yes, but you're wearing a yellow jersey, and Hero doesn't like yellow. Whip it off and he'll be fine with you."

"Huh?" Peter demanded, looking from Sergei to Hero.

"Lots of animals don't like yellow. In fact, if you ask humans their favorite color, it's rare you'll hear yellow from them, either. We're animals, after all."

"That's weird!" Eddie declared, glancing at his own purple jersey, crossing his arms, and staring at Hero.

"Very weird," Cal agreed as he rested a tattooed arm on Eddie's head.

Jake watched Peter take off his yellow jersey, hide it behind his motorcycle, and approach Hero. Hero blinked at Peter a few times, then slowly lowered his muzzle toward Peter's face. He tolerated Peter raising his hand and touching his nose.

"He likes me now!" Peter declared, grinning triumphantly. "I'm part of the herd."

"Okay, everyone," Sergei said. "We've learned sidehilling, we've survived one crash, and we've visited Back-of-Beyond Ranch's guard llama. Dana and her crew will soon be at the cabin waiting to eat lunch with us, and Hero needs to get back to work looking after the sheep. So, let's get going. Going up the hill will be easier than coming down. Just pick a gear and stick with it so you avoid shifting gears. And use your body to maintain traction. No wheelying, and definitely no more endos." He smiled at Jake.

Everyone nodded. Jake stretched his stiff body and climbed back on his bike. One by one, they worked their way back up the hill, then hit the trail, letting the dust fly. After half an hour, the trail grew a little easier as it approached the point where the Forest Service A-frame cabin sat. Several hours from the time they'd left the ranch, they roared up to it and cut their motors. The llama cart was parked neatly in front.

"Can't wait to eat! I'm starved," Peter announced as he placed his helmet on the front steps and peeled off his sweaty jersey.

"I'll be back in a minute," Jake replied. "Gotta use the outhouse."

He placed his helmet beside Peter's and turned up a path as the rest of the dirt-bike team bounded up the cabin steps. Jake heard Cal greet his wife and daughter and Peter shout, "Alright! Look at all these sandwiches and cookies! Natalia's been busy!"

When he reached the outhouse, Jake noticed that its door, sporting a carved half moon, was closed.

"Anyone there?" He leaned down and saw no legs in the gap between the door and its sill. He tried the door and found it unlocked. But when he pulled it open, his hand went to his mouth and he backed away.

Sitting cross-legged on top of the toilet's closed lid was Dana. Her eyes were fastened on her arm, which was raised in front of her as she slid a needle into her skin.

Not until she was finished did she look at him. Her cold eyes revealed neither shame nor fear, just annoyance that he'd barged in on her. She said nothing. But the brief, chilly flick of her eyes over him told him in no uncertain terms that he was to beat it, now.

Jake spun around and ran for the cabin.

8   Spokane

Five days later, Peter stepped out of Sergei's four-wheel-drive truck, his pulse quickening at the sights, smells, and sounds of the moto.

Motorcycles of every size were zipping up and down the outdoor course on practise runs. They whined like a forest full of loggers whose chainsaws were starting, stopping, accelerating, and dying, each to their own schedule. The overall chorus was deafening, out of tune, and chaotic.

Peter sprinted to the fence and jumped up and down, arms high in the air. "Yes! Look at that lead guy, Jake! Whoa! Did you see him jump the gap? Whoopee! Awesome!"

"He's good, alright," Jake responded as he, Dana, and Sergei joined Peter at the fence.

Rear tires spewed plumes of dirt into the air as helmeted bodies in bright jerseys and pants flew past.

They rounded banked turns with heads bent forward, gloved hands clutching controls, knees hugging their machines. A portion of the dust kicked up refused to settle back into the track's ruts. Instead, it dispersed slowly over the crowds, lodging in Peter's eyes, nostrils, throat, and pores. It nearly blocked out the smell of hotdogs at a nearby stand. Rock music, which Peter knew would be turned up during halftime, played over the loudspeakers.

Beside the boys and Dana, parents of the competitors cheered, shouted tips, and chatted in clusters along a low chain-link fence. Others sat in open-air bleachers near the middle of the course. Many held brooms, which they waved up and down when their kids passed by.

"What's with the brooms?" Jake asked Peter.

"Parents use them to sweep the starting gate for their kid," Peter replied. "Otherwise, when the starting gate drops, the rear tires may spin because they're sliding on the dust instead of getting traction on the concrete."

"Did we bring a broom?"

"I did," Dana replied from behind them.

Peter turned to her. "You doing the girl's-class race *and* the halftime freestyle competition?"

She nodded, eyes on the racers.

"Girl's class any good?"

She shrugged. Peter looked to Jake as if hoping for a translation. Jake had recently claimed that Dana had a dozen different kinds of shrugs, each with its own meaning. Peter hadn't decided if Jake was pulling his leg or was onto something.

"If none of the pros are here, Dana's top of her class," Sergei pronounced.

"Yeah?" Peter felt himself bristle. He and Jake exchanged looks. Peter knew they were both wondering how a druggie could be a good racer, and whether Sergei knew. Peter decided to block it from his mind for now.

"Nice track, yes?" Sergei said. "Four double jumps." He pointed to six-foot-high piles of dirt with forty-foot gaps between them. "Keep your weight centered, your elbows and knees bent, and your eyes straight ahead on those," he advised.

Peter jabbed a finger at the giant dirt hills skimmed flat at the top. He pictured running up the steep slope, then catching air to sail across the horizontal top and land ready to start down the far slope of the pile. "Five tabletops on this course. On those, we jump front wheel high, right?"

"You got it." Sergei turned his head to the right and pointed to a section of much smaller hills: speed bump-like moguls. "The tabletops will be challenging, but it's the whoops where you're going to win or lose, boys. Skim the front tire from peak to peak if you can. It's all in the body position."

Peter eyed the whoops.

"Body position?" Jake asked, sweaty fingers curled around the chain-link fence.

"Let your body be the shock absorber," Peter explained. He saw Jake nod, but his friend's eyes looked clouded, as if he was trying to take in too much information at once.

"How come you don't have whoops on the track up at the ranch?" Jake asked Sergei.

"Because he's Russian," Dana said before Sergei could answer. Peter turned and saw a rare sparkle in her eyes, as if she was proud of beating Sergei to the answer. "They don't usually have whoops in Europe."

"But this is Washington state," Peter said. "We need them to practise on."

"I've told him," Dana said, smiling at Sergei.

"*Gloopy* things, whoops," Sergei said.

Peter laughed. He liked the Russian word for "silly."

"No, Sergei, *not* having whoops to practise on is *gloopy*," Jake corrected him.

But Sergei had craned his head and was watching a flock of 80s ridden by youngsters half Jake's and Peter's size come careening down the nearest section of the course. He frowned deeply. "Bateman brats," he mumbled. "All three of 'em." Then he shrugged. "Okay kids, let's get these bikes out of the truck, get suited up and registered, and do our practise run. Race starts in an hour and a half."

Within twenty minutes, Peter was tearing up the course, going for speed up the hills, whipping it on jumps where he needed to slow himself as he caught air. He saw Jake fail to pour on enough speed to make the top of the second hill. His buddy gassed it but wasn't standing high enough on the tank. Peter winced as Jake rolled upside down onto his back. Knowing that Jake would be winded but would pick himself up and carry on, Peter roared on ahead, just behind Dana. When he saw Dana take the first double-jump gap, Peter hefted his own 125 into the air. When he saw her corner on the inside of a bank, he followed suit. As he sped up to pass her on a straightaway, he saw her front tire catch in a rut and take her down in a cloud of dust. He veered around her just in time. Well, too bad for her, he thought. Since girls had their own class, he wouldn't be competing against her. Which was probably a good thing. He grabbed a handful of throttle up the next tabletop, leapt to its far side, and completed his first lap in decent time. Decent, but not impressive.

By his fifth time around the mile-and-a-half loop, Peter had it dialed. He'd also had time to check out the other racers his age. There were twenty in his class, the 125 juniors. Two dudes he had no chance of beating, he figured, but that was okay. The one closest to his skill level was wearing a green jersey emblazoned with his name and number: "Levi, No. 118." Peter figured he had an outside chance of beating out this Levi guy if he had a good run. That meant acing everything while going at the highest speed he could handle, for all fifteen minutes, or roughly seven laps, of the moto. As for the rest of the pack, including Jake—who'd bitten the dust at least once on each lap so far—they existed merely for passing.

Peter headed back to the "pit" that Sergei had established for them. Jake was there already, motorcycle up on a stand, head bent over his front forks.

"I'm adjusting my suspension for better performance on the whoops," he told Peter around the screwdriver in his mouth. "You should try it, too."

"Maybe," said Peter, bike still idling.

Sergei was pulling a soda out of the ice chest. Dana was talking to a man and woman Peter had never seen before.

"Peter, you're looking good out there," Sergei said as Peter cut his motor. "Come meet Dana's parents."

Dana's parents? Peter looked at them with curiosity. Her mother had Dana's fit-looking build and the same dark, curly hair. She wore no makeup and had the bookish look of a librarian. Her dad looked like a weather-beaten farmer, even if he'd given up farming: he wore faded blue jeans, a workshirt, and suspenders. He was glancing around the pits as if he'd rather be anywhere but this noisy place.

"Hi," Peter said, extending his hand. "I'm Peter, one of the junior guides at Back-of-Beyond."

"Hi," Dana's father and mother said at the same time before Dana's mother returned to her conversation with Dana.

"I hear you used to be a llama farmer," Peter addressed Dana's dad.

"Yup," he said, hooking his thumbs around his suspenders. "Don't miss it. Too much work, not enough money. Dana misses it something terrible, though. So she was pretty happy to hook up with Sergei. Glad you all came into town so we could see her. How's she doing up there on the ranch?"

Peter glanced at Dana and her mother, who were moving toward the refreshment stand, still chatting. "Fine, I guess, not that she says much," Peter commented, turning his eyes back to her father for his reaction to that.

Dana's father smiled. "That one never has said much," he said. "Guess it's our fault, raising an only child on an isolated farm and letting her spend all her time with the llamas. It probably didn't help that my wife agreed to home-school her when she refused to bus to school any more."

"Refused to bus to school?" Peter asked, checking to make sure that Dana and her mother were well out of earshot.

"Yeah, you know how mean kids can be when someone's a little different. They didn't understand, and Dana was still trying to figure out her problem. She couldn't handle their teasing. So the home-schooling made sense at first. We've just never gotten around to getting her back in school. Guess that hasn't helped her shyness. Maybe being around you boys will loosen her up this summer."

"Yeah, maybe," Peter said, confused but not wanting to be nosey, and definitely not wanting Dana to overhear any further conversation. Different? Problem? Did Dana's dad know she did drugs?

"She's sure not shy on a dirt bike," Peter offered.

Dana's father threw his head back and laughed. "No, that's the one place my girl has never been shy—on dirt bikes!" He extended his hand. "Well, better see what my wife and Dana are up to. Good luck on your race, son. Dana says you're pretty good."

9   Moto

Half an hour later, Peter and Jake were lined up at the starting gate as Sergei vigorously swept their concrete pads for them.

A dirty-faced kid maybe eleven years old approached. "Hey Sergei, can we borrow your broom during the 80cc meet? We forgot ours."

Peter watched Sergei turn and his eyes slant as he surveyed the kid. The kid looked too old for an 80. Peter guessed he was one of those boys without enough money to trade up yet.

"Since when do you 'borrow' anything, Chuck Bateman?" he growled. "You steal my gas again and you'll be seeing this broom in full use."

Peter looked over at Jake, who raised his eyebrows at Peter. Whoa, that was pretty direct, Peter thought. But Chuck didn't look intimidated. He sneered, spun on his boot heel, and disappeared.

Sergei finished sweeping Jake's and Peter's pads. "Go like stink!" the Russian said, grinning widely. "And remember, it's okay to talk to your machines."

Talk to your machines? Peter grinned and rolled his eyes at Jake, who smiled back at him.

As the lineup of bikers revved their engines to clear out unburned fuel, Peter's nostrils stung with the smell of exhaust, and his ears rang inside his helmet. He looked over at Jake and gave him a thumbs-up. Jake gave him a hesitant smile.

Poor Jake. He'd rather be in the pits, Peter knew, but racing would make him a better mechanic. Peter looked over at Levi, the guy he wanted to beat. He caught Levi's dark and not unfriendly eyes checking him out before the boy's shiny green helmet turned straight ahead.

The five-second sign came up, then the metal gates dropped, and the motorbikes smoked off their pads. Peter gunned for the holeshot, missed it, and slid into the pack somewhere around fifth. He found himself immediately behind Levi.

Up the first hill they went, some competitors sailing high and others low over the crest before tearing down the far side. Ruts, rocks, and rooster tails of dirt flew at Peter. He leaned, shifted, and swayed with the demands of the terrain. As the pack spread out, he set his jaw and kept his eyes on No. 118.

Peter took the first tabletop cautiously, landing just short of its far slope. The touchdown jarred and nearly tossed him, but he held tight. No way was he going to be bucked off on the first jump. Next time he'd be bolder.

As he approached the next section, the whoops, he felt his hands tighten on their controls. Ahead, bikes leapt and landed like sandflies on a beach. Skim, skim, jump. Jump, dip, skim. Each competitor attacked the whoops differently, the best ones pulling ahead. Someone's back tire hit a rut and the bike looped out, causing a small pile-up behind him. The rest of the pack veered to pass them like a wave splitting on a jetty.

Skim, skim, jump. Peter's body became a giant shock absorber. He hit the crests like a Jet Ski might plow through wave tips. But there was nothing soft or wet about these billows; the dust of the course coated his dry mouth, and even his bones seemed to reverberate. Beyond the whoops, the course became more rutted with every lap. Peter passed one hole large enough to fit his entire bike into. He hoped the course grooming people would fill it in during halftime.

At every corner he could see he was closing the gap between him and Levi. Soon they were battling it out, leapfrogging past each other from one section to another. It made Peter's adrenalin flow. Every racer likes "a good dice," motocross talk for a duel. One lap, two laps. Definitely giving No. 118 a run for his money. Peter gave Jake wide berth as he passed him on the third lap. Jake, old buddy, you're still doing your second lap, he thought. Oh well, at least you're still on your bike. But gun it, bro. Nothing to fear but fear itself.

As Peter shot into the air over a double, he saw a yellow flag. Oops. That meant someone had gone down just ahead. He veered right, narrowly missing the racer, who was struggling to stand and kick-start his bike again. Peter's jerky detour put him elbow-to-elbow with a competitor attempting to pass him. Oh no you don't. As they headed around a berm, Peter dared to speed up and ride high. Yikes! A dirt clod appeared out of nowhere, knocking his front wheel to the right. As his bike wobbled, Peter kicked out a leg, but it was too late. He skidded, went over the handlebars, did a face plant. He tucked his arms in, knowing that others could land on him. Luckily, no one did. He jumped up, hopped back in his saddle, and kicked the kick-starter. He kicked again. Nothing. He cursed, and tried again. This time it roared to life. Off he went, tearing after the now faraway pack. The incident had cost him—Levi must be cruising past the checkered flag about now—but he was still in the game. As he flew to his finish, he reminded himself it was only the first moto. He had one more this afternoon to up his points. Hopefully he'd still have plenty of energy after the halftime's freestyle event.

"How'd it go?" he asked Jake as he pulled into the pits.

"I'm a disaster on the jumps," Jake admitted.

"It's like Sergei said," Peter encouraged him, laying a hand on his padded shoulders. "Weight centered, elbows and knees bent, eyes straight ahead."

"Yeah. So did you set your suspension like I suggested?"

"Not yet, old buddy. Gotta get some food in me first."

"Dana and Sergei both won their motos," Jake reported.

"We did but it's a long day, with lots of racing left, Jake," Sergei said with a grin. "Anything can happen this afternoon. Grab a sandwich before your halftime show, Peter and Dana."

Peter needed no further urging, but he noticed that Dana went right to retuning her bike.

"Dana, eat something," Sergei coaxed her sternly.

"In a minute," she said, her head bent to her carburetor.

Not that it was Peter's business, but he noticed she still hadn't eaten anything by the time they had to motor over to the freestyle section. He also thought she looked a little pale and sweaty. Dana, nervous? Or did she need a fix? He looked at Dana, her face intent on the bike, and couldn't believe this girl had a drug problem.

"Did you eat any lunch?" he ventured.

She turned startled eyes on him. "What are you, my mother? I ate something a while back. If I eat right before I race, when I'm nervous, it knots up my stomach."

"Makes sense," Peter said. "Sorry, wasn't my business."

He turned as he heard a catchy rock tune blare full-blast from the speakers. "They're gearing up for halftime!" he said, wandering away.

"Welcome to the halftime freestyle show! Find a seat!" the announcer on the public address system was saying twenty minutes later. He was referring to a small section of metal bleachers just off the outdoor track. "You can have a whole seat, but you'll only need the edge of one for this event! Five of the biggest, best riders in Washington state are here to show you a good time. Watch 'em shoot thirty feet into the air and seventy-five feet across gaps. Ladies and gentlemen, big air, big applause …"

Peter, feet splayed each side of his machine, pulled his hands out of his gloves to wipe them on the seat of his pants as he waited his turn in line. The first guy gunned his motorcycle, rode casually to the ramp, and shot up it like a high diver about to plunge into a pool. As his bike leveled out high over the site, he whipped it sideways, took a foot off a peg, and stabbed it crookedly backwards. An awkward Nac-Nac, to Peter's eye, but the guy landed and the crowd erupted into cheers.

"That was Fernando Valerto, only thirteen years old, our youngest competitor today," the announcer enthused. "He's going to set the freestyle world on fire …"

Fernando, Peter mused. A pushy little kid with big ambitions. Totally unpopular with other MXers. Known among MXers as "The Brat." "The Brat" had an archrival who was also here today. Honza Vozanilek was worse than bratty; he could be vicious and nasty both on and off the course. And he was as good at freestyle as he was at motocross racing.

"Honza is approaching the ramp," the announcer was saying. "Dressed head to toe in red and really speeding up on that new red bike of his. Do you like those little horns he's attached to his helmet? What a showman! Let's see what devilish tricks he's going to show us today!"

Peter watched Honza glide effortlessly up the ramp, then take both feet off his pegs. In one smooth motion, he stood on the forward portion of his seat for a second, bent forward so that his hands still gripped his handlebars. Then he lifted his entire body up and back, all on the strength of his arms and shoulders, until from helmet to boots his body hung like a smile above the airborne bike. It was as if he was flying, with only his hands on the handlebars connecting with the bike. All he needed was a cape to truly look like Superman, which is what the trick was called. An intermediate trick requiring lots of upper body strength, well performed, Peter allowed.

The crowd cheered.

As the next freestyler motored toward the ramp, he veered suddenly and circled back, head low. "It's okay, folks," the announcer said. "He'll take another run at it in a minute. This is Hseuh-yi Koo, also known as the Comeback Kid. Injured his back last year, did some time in a wheelchair, but hasn't let it hold him back. He's determined to reclaim his title today. Let's give him some encouragement."

Peter watched as Hseuh-yi sped up the ramp on his second go. In mid-air, he started to lay his entire body back on the seat, probably going for a Lazy-Boy. But he aborted it and slid back into position just in time to land a little sketchily. Poor guy.

"It's okay, Hseuh-yi. Folks, he didn't find what he was looking for that time, but I have a feeling he's going to pull out all the stops on the next round. Now, next up is our only female competitor, long-time local freestyler Dana Young."

Peter gripped his handlebars as he watched Dana fly up the ramp. He glued his eyes on her as she leveled her bike, slipped her leg over the seat, and extended it to the opposite side of the motorcycle. Neat and well practised, perfect balance. Her Can-Can was good, the best trick yet. But Peter's right hand was already working his throttle.

"Peter Montpetit from Seattle is a newcomer to our scene, but word has it he's hot. Look at him take that ramp, folks. Whoa, a Double Can-Can, first move. Here's someone worth keeping an eye on. Let's put our hands together for Peter Montpetit …"

Face sticky inside his helmet, Peter grinned as he executed a perfect landing. One trick down, two to go. Was he up for trying his backflip?

Lined up for the second trick, Peter watched Dana pull her helmet off, wipe an arm across her forehead, and put it back on. Then she lowered her head onto her handlebars as if it was too heavy to hold up. "You okay, Dana?" he asked. "Your Can-Can was good."

She turned and looked at him. Her mouth seemed drawn, and perspiration trickled down her neck. She nodded, but her eyes had a clouded look.

"Dana Young again, folks. Let's see what she's going to give us this time."

Dana's right heel lifted to kick-start her engine. Her bike lurched forward and headed for the ramp. As she lifted skyward, she raised both boots at the same time, then kicked them straight back on one side. Although Peter expected her to re-straddle the seat before landing, she stayed side-saddle even as the bike cruised toward the far side of the dirt pile.

"Yes! Look at that, ladies and gentlemen. What a showgirl. A Double Can-Can with an Annie Oakley landing from our very own Dana."

Peter exhaled slowly. She'd been nervous, close to totally psyched out, if he hadn't been seeing things, but she'd pulled it off. He gritted his teeth and fired up his bike. He shot up the ramp and bought as much air as he could. He lifted his feet past his handlebars, and with a death grip on them, lowered his back all the way to his seat. The first time he'd tried a Lazy-Boy, he'd decided it was well named. Just like what his dad did in his favorite chair in front of the television on Sundays.

"What an acrobat! A stunning Lazy-Boy from ..."

Peter blocked the announcer's noise from his brain as he landed the trick and rode back around to the lineup. Now he was going to have to totally concentrate. Time to contemplate his third and last trick. He'd never done a backflip outside of the pool, but he'd been landing four out of five there. "It's time," he told himself.

He played a reel in his head of himself acing it. He played it again and again. He pictured himself collecting the $100 prize money. He could do it. He was concentrating so hard as he waited in the lineup that he hardly noticed The Brat's Pendulum or Honza's Seat-Grab or the Comeback Kid's perfect backflip. He was concentrating so hard, he barely registered the crowd's roar after Dana shot up in the air and disappeared from his view. He was vaguely aware that people in the stands had risen to their feet. She must have done something really special. He waited for his signal, waited and waited. He was ready; why was the signal taking so long?

Finally! He sped up the ramp, flew high, and pulled up, up, up. There was a crucial split second he had to pull his bike from up to over. That's the split second Sergei would've had him talk to his bike, communicate with its "soul." Which was hogwash, of course, and not something Peter was about to do thirty feet over the ground with hundreds of eyes on him. But maybe the bike talked to him that instant. Maybe its engine emitted the tiniest of coughs. Somehow, Peter just knew to abort the smooth loop he'd envisioned. He kept the bike sailing upright. Somehow, like the Comeback Kid on his first try, he knew it wasn't time right then. His hopes for the prize fell at the same rate as the bike. He knew that the half-hearted Heel Click he did was a pretty pale substitute for the perfect backflip he'd planned as he took to the air. But backflips require 110 percent commitment. Something had yanked his commitment away. So he'd done the next best thing, which was to follow his instincts and prevent a crash that could've caused serious injury.

As his rear, then front tire touched down, he expected cheering even if his trick had been a little lame. He was, after all, rolling, rolling down the slope, steady and smooth and a probable second-place finisher.

So why wasn't the crowd cheering for him?

He looked ahead, saw Sergei running toward him, but Sergei didn't look happy. He saw Dana's parents at Sergei's heels. He saw Sergei stop and kneel beside Dana. What was Dana doing lying on the ground beside her bike, eyes trained on the sky? He saw Sergei place his big arm under Dana's neck and lift her head. Saw Sergei push a carton of orange juice to Dana's lips. Saw medics running and Dana's mom unzip Dana's fanny pack to pull out a syringe, but Sergei waved it away.

"It's okay," Sergei was saying to the medics. "She's diabetic. I'm a doctor—I mean a vet. She must have forgotten to eat lunch, but I can tell we've got it in time."

Peter watched Dana's mom study Dana, then nod agreement and tuck the syringe back in the bag.

"Thank you, Sergei," Dana's mother said, her voice so steady that Peter could only assume she'd been through this many times.

"Dana, Dana," Sergei was saying. "Good girl, you're going to be okay."

10   Second Heat

"**Y**our friend okay?"

Jake was lined up at the restrooms when he turned to see a guy in a green jersey addressing him.

"Yeah, she's okay," he responded, sizing up the guy. Someone from the 125 junior division, his and Peter's age. His number plate was No. 118. He vaguely remembered Peter being neck and neck with him for a while this morning. Like most of the racers, he was someone who had passed Jake early on. "She's just resting up. She's diabetic, I just found out. I guess that means if she doesn't eat regularly, her blood sugar gets low and she can go into shock or something."

"Yeah, I remember her from when she used to go to our school. She has to prick her finger a coupla times a day and test her blood on some little gizmo and sometimes give herself injections of insulin. The kids used to give her a hard time about it."

Jake nodded soberly as he pictured Dana, cross-legged in the outhouse, poking a needle into her own arm. Gross. He couldn't imagine doing that, let alone several times a day, but maybe you'd get used to it. Guess you had to, if you wanted to live. Weird. He was still trying to take it all in. How come no one had told Peter and him that Dana had a medical problem? Then again, why would they? He remembered Natalia baking bread and making Peter deliver it to Dana. What was it Natalia had said to Sergei that day? "She forgets to eat sometimes, and then it is trouble …"

Well, for someone about to go into insulin shock, or whatever they called it, Dana sure had performed well at halftime. The judges had said her Can-Can and Double Can-Can were excellent. If she hadn't slid off her bike after landing her third trick, she might even have taken the prize. Peter's nose was going to be out of joint for not getting that prize. But that's what he got for being a little full of himself. The Comeback Kid had come back to a first place standing after all. Peter had clinched second. Jake had watched that announcement prompt a major scowl on The Brat's face. Brat's arch competitor, Honza, the one with the stupid devil's horns on his helmet, had closed his eyes and punched his fist into a concrete wall. The blood on his knuckles had perfectly matched his red outfit and motorcycle.

"Grow up," Jake had muttered out of earshot at the time.

"I'm Levi Morgan," the boy in the green jersey said, extending his hand. "Nice to have some new guys in the 125 junior division."

"Thanks," Jake replied. "Oh, here's Peter." He guessed that Peter, like him, had wandered over to give Sergei, Dana, and her parents some privacy. As Jake had left the pits, they'd been settling Dana on the bed in her parents' camper. She'd looked embarrassed and dazed. He was glad Peter had followed him over so they could talk about it. Could talk about it, that is, when Levi wasn't around. "Peter, this is Levi."

Jake watched Peter give Levi the once-over before raising his hand. "Hi. Been racing long?"

"Since I was seven on a mini," Levi said, smiling. "And you?"

"A few years," Peter said.

"No way."

"Well, I went to a camp that taught it last summer. Got some pretty intense coaching."

"Camp must've been good." Levi seemed genuinely friendly, Jake decided. "Sweet freestyle move out there."

"Nah, I sucked," Peter said, shoulders hunched.

"No, really. Good stuff. You guys work up at Back-of-Beyond Ranch, someone told me. With Sergei, the rancher guy who won this morning's masters class?"

"Yup."

"Nice. My dad's booked us for some trails up there next week. Including an overnight to a cabin. Is it true there's a full motocross track up there, too?"

"Everything on it but whoops," Jake confirmed.

"Must be tough, a summer job like that." He grinned. "Well, see you at the starting gate in an hour."

"See you," Jake and Peter answered together.

"So," Jake turned to Peter, "poor Dana."

"Yeah. Good thing she didn't hurt herself, and that Sergei had that orange juice on him. He says orange juice has tons of sugar in it, and that he keeps some around for when she does this. She gets lightheaded and loses coordination if she hasn't tested herself and eaten or given herself a shot in time."

"Yeah, and sometimes he has to give her an injection if she's left it so late she's too out of it. She always keeps a whole kit of syringes and stuff in her fanny pack. I guess being a vet, Sergei knows how to give shots."

Peter scratched his head. "Hadn't thought of that, though I don't know if animals get diabetes."

Jake smiled. "Actually, Sergei says they do. Anyway, glad it wasn't what we thought about her."

"Yeah, she's not that type. But how were we supposed to know?"

They were now halfway back to the pits. "Peter," Jake started in, "have you re-jetted your bike yet? Your bike is running a bit rough. You probably flooded it when you spilled on the corner during the first heat. You're lucky it didn't act up on you during the freestyle stunts. It'll only take a minute to fix it."

"You want to do it?" Peter asked.

"Sergei says I'm supposed to make you do your own maintenance. And he's back at the pits, so he'll yell at me if he sees me do it."

"Yeah, okay." Peter scowled.

"Good. Want some ice cream from the stand?" Jake figured Peter would be finished with his repair by the time Jake returned with the ice cream.

"You bet. It's getting grossly hot this afternoon."

"More humid. Like it's going to rain." Jake looked at the sky, saw gray clouds approaching.

Peter looked up and frowned. "Thought it hardly ever rained in eastern Washington."

"Guess 'hardly ever' doesn't mean never. A downpour might do interesting things to those ruts." Jake tightened his jaw as he gazed at the sky, then at the course.

"Way too interesting," Peter agreed, eyebrows knit.

Ten minutes later, Jake returned to the pits to find

Peter, Sergei, and Dana's dad struggling to tie a tarp over the camping chairs. The sky looked ready to let loose any time. Dana's mom was chopping fruit inside the camper. Dana was lying on the camper's bed, propped up on one elbow, popping grapes into her mouth.

Jake passed one ice cream cone to Peter. He paused in the camper's doorway to finish off his own.

"How're you feeling?" Her face had color again. But Sergei had told the boys that after an insulin reaction, Dana was usually wiped out for a couple of hours.

"Fine, but I have to DNF." Jake knew that stood for "did not finish." He hadn't expected anyone to allow her to do the afternoon moto.

"Bummer."

"Yeah." Her eyes studied the floor of the camper, then rose to his face. "How's it going for you?"

"I think I'm getting the hang of it. Or at least I will be by the end of my second moto."

"Good." She lifted the bowl of grapes toward him.

"Thanks." A rain splatter hit his upturned face just before he moved further inside the camper. "At least you don't have to bike in the rain," he said.

"Mmmm," she said.

"Mmmm?" he mimicked her with a grin. "I'm Jake, not Furball. It's okay to use words. Though I like the way llamas hum."

He saw a hint of a smile form around the grape going into her mouth. "Biking in mud is sketchy," she declared.

"Yeah? Got some special tips? So I don't come dead last, that is."

"It turns things slippery fast. It kills your momentum, gloms onto your bike, and weighs it down."

"Wonderful."

"Stiffen your suspension a little and gear down a tooth or two."

Jake thought for a moment, tried to picture some stuff in a book he'd been reading. "How about if I spray silicone on my ignition cover and under my fenders to stop mud from collecting? I think I also read somewhere you can put a zip tie around the base of the spark plug cap."

She studied him. "A zip tie? You are a serious motorhead."

Jake smiled. Zip ties, those little plastic strips most people used to close up their garbage bags, could be formed into loops and pulled tightly around engine parts.

"Of course, mechanics isn't everything. Even serious motorheads can talk to their bikes. At least, that's what Sergei would suggest."

Jake studied her but couldn't tell if she was serious or mocking their boss. They looked up as a clatter sounded on the camper's roof.

"Will you listen to that downpour?" Dana's mother exclaimed. "My goodness! No one should be biking out there in this! And Jake, I know Dana is enjoying your company, but I'm thinking maybe she needs to be resting more."

"I am resting, Mom." Dana sat up, squinted at the water dripping past the camper's open door, then pulled her blanket up to her chin.

"Nearly time for your last heat, Jake."

Jake checked his watch. "Yup, but just enough time to fiddle with my bike first."

"Excuse me." It was a small voice. Jake looked down to see a mud-spattered boy in ripped motocross gear, looking up at him. The kid was no more than nine.

"Yes?" Jake asked, resisting a smile.

"Could I borrow your crescent wrench? My dad forgot his, and I gotta fix my 80 before the next moto."

Jake looked at the kid and his big eyes. Cute. Amazing at what a young age kids started motocross these days. The next Ricky Carmichaels. Maybe Jake would be better at the sport if he'd started that young. Jake fished through his tool box to produce the crescent wrench when he heard Dana's voice call out from the trailer.

"Liam Bateman! Scram!" Her no-nonsense voice

made the kid start. Big eyes looked into the trailer, looked back at Jake, looked longingly at the wrench.

Jake hesitated. But before he could make up his mind, Liam had turned and run, splashing up mud on whatever portions of himself weren't already dark with dirt.

It took Jake fifteen minutes to set up for riding in the mud. He'd have instructed Peter how to do it too if Peter hadn't disappeared. As Jake finished up, he spotted his buddy at Levi's pit, holding what looked like a lively discussion.

The rain hadn't eased by the time Jake motored toward the starting gates. The last moto. And it was going to be a mud bath.

A few minutes later, Peter showed up. "Good luck, old buddy," Peter said as he positioned his bike and stared ahead at the course.

"Same." Jake raised his head to study the first jump. It was the one that got him every time. Why couldn't he just shoot up and over the lip like everyone else? He knew he needed more speed, but last time, he'd gunned it too much. That had made him over-shoot, panic, and wipe out. He couldn't seem to get it just right. He'd just about figured out the whoops. Why was he still choking on the double jumps? Why couldn't he be like Peter?

When the starting gate dropped, Jake went only

half throttle. He didn't want to be in the middle of a tight pack on the first curve, especially as the rain turned portions of the track into brown soup. He also didn't want to get run over when he blew it on the hill. He didn't want to be last, but if he had no chance of being out in front, he might as well aim for finishing without a spill. For once.

The first hill came at him as if it was rising up out of the earth. Head forward, knees tense, breathing hard, Jake tried to remember Peter's advice. Was it "stay centered" or "lean forward"? He tried leaning forward, felt his bike start to lose it. His stomach tightened as he kicked his legs out in a desperate attempt to keep his balance. Weaving like a drunk, his motorcycle zoomed up the slippery slope and over the summit. His wrists pushed down as he decided his front tire had come up too high. Wham! Bike and boy hit the downslope, fishtailed, then steadied. Okay, he was still on the bike. No faceful of mud or yellow flag yet. But next time he'd listen harder to Peter. Must've said "stay centered," not "lean forward." He smiled. Jake Evans, folks, by a stroke of luck and balance, has just been promoted from "Disaster" to "Competent." Can he, will he, steer himself into the "Competitive" class?

He hugged a wet corner, dared to pass a straggler. Confidence rising, he got up the courage to accelerate on the straightaway. The rain was steady now, cool on his skin as it soaked through his jersey. The track had the smell of newly dampened dirt.

Jake glued his eyes to the track. Whoops up next. Crest to crest to crest. Keep those tires out of the dips, which were turning into watery ditches, and keep those eyes glued ahead. Bam, bam, bam. Is that all you've got, you stupid whoops? Bring it on! Me and my bike can take it. Jake gritted his teeth as he whomped, whomped, whomped over them. His body, jaw, and machine were reverberating like a milkshake in a shake machine.

There! Free of the whoops, coming to a tabletop. Tabletops are okay, he reminded himself. Ready, attack, go! Wheee! As Jake came sailing down, he felt as if someone had turned on the showerhead full blast. This was turning into one wet race. As he dodged a stone, a rooster tail of mud landed on his goggles. On the next jump, he reached up and ripped off one of his tear-offs, thin plastic lenses snapped into place over goggles to allow a rider to clear his vision in such conditions. As racers slipped and fell around him, Jake stayed the course, his gear two teeth below what he'd normally choose, just as Dana had suggested.

Though he had limited visibility in this rain shower, he managed to avoid being part of a pack that went down together. They were writhing in the mud like pigs on a pig farm. Jake hoped Peter wasn't among them. A few bodies managed to extract themselves from the mud bath and climb back on their bogged-down bikes. But by then, Jake was chugging past them, slow but steady, a smaller pack of competitors now in front of him. As he zoomed past the black and white checkers, he raised a triumphant fist and steered toward his pit. Yes! He'd finished middle instead of near the end of the pack. It was all thanks to the fiddling he'd done to give his bike extra protection against the wet. Well, okay, and maybe a little luck.

Thank goodness he had Dana's dry camper to climb into to change. Better than the cab of Sergei's 4WD.

"Hey, Dana, feeling better? Where's Peter?" Jake asked as he drew up.

She laughed to see him covered head to toe in mud. Her mother beamed beside her. "I'm good. Way drier than you. How'd you do?" Dana asked.

"Middle." He shrugged.

"That's good, Jake. You must've passed quite a few to pull that off. Peter's over grumping with his new friend."

"Huh?"

Dana tossed him a towel as he stood on the steps of the trailer. "Sergei says Peter finally managed to pass

No. 118 ten minutes in, but Peter's rear shock started to fade. He ended up going down."

"And Levi went down with him?"

"If Levi is No. 118, yes. He was right behind. He didn't have a chance."

"That means Peter didn't do the suspension adjustments like I told him to. I knew that would happen! I warned him! That lazy punk! I bet Levi is pretty angry."

Dana shrugged. "Doesn't look angry to me. Crashes happen. No one was hurt."

Jake felt Sergei's hand on his shoulder. "Hey, Jake."

Jake grinned. "Hi, Sergei. Way to win the masters class again."

"Thanks. Nice work yourself, even if you nearly blew it on the first double."

Jake sighed. "Yeah, I couldn't remember what Peter told me to do there."

"Just like Peter managed to overlook what you told him," Sergei said, tsk-tsking like Natalia. "*Gloopy* boys. It's like I said. Technique *and* maintenance. Body and soul. One is no good without the other."

"*Da*," Jake agreed, sighing again. All he knew was that his body was too drenched, and his soul too tired, to argue with a crazy Russian.

11 Whoops

"**M**y cheese soufflé! It is fallen!" cried Natalia as she yanked open the oven door, tottering on the high heels of her knee-high leather boots. "This oven, she is ...!"

Jake smiled at Peter as the heat escaping from the oven traveled to his nostrils, bringing with it a delicious whiff of Natalia's fluffy cheese-and-egg dish. Peter grinned at Sergei. Sergei winked at Levi and his dad, Jerry Morgan, whose faces relaxed as they registered that there was no crisis, that they were merely in on some sort of normal routine here at the big ranch house.

"Natalia, it smells *v'koosna*," Jake reassured her, proud he'd learned the word for "tasty" from Sergei and pleased that he and Peter had been invited to the big house for a real dinner. Natalia was wearing a leather miniskirt and a light cotton sweater, all covered by her spotless chef's apron.

"*Nyet, nyet*, it is too flat," Natalia said, shaking her head as she steered it toward the table between her giant oven mitts.

"Not as flat as Levi's tire went on the trail today when he tried to cross a creek," Sergei joked. "Lucky for him Jake had a patch in his fanny pack."

"Hard to see sharp rocks when your tire is underwater," Levi spoke up. "But I'd have changed it myself if Jake had let me. He was too fast." The boy handed a platter of buttered asparagus to Jake.

"He's faster at tire changes than riding in motos, but we'll train him up, Levi," Peter offered as the soufflé dish finally came his way.

Jake sighed, but he was too busy tucking into his dinner to take Peter's bait.

"That's quite the track you have up here," said Jerry. "It's got everything but whoops."

"It could have whoops if Sergei would let us use his Bobcat," Jake suggested, referring to the little earthmover Sergei kept around for farmwork. "And we could make the double jump higher, too—as high as the ones at the moto in Spokane. The rain has made the ground nice and soft to work with. Maybe Levi would like to help us, since you guys are up here for a few days."

"I'd be into that," Levi said, glancing at Jake and

Peter as if making sure they were serious.

"Me too," Jerry offered, then sneezed and tugged a handkerchief from his pocket. "Or maybe not. I've been feeling off my game for a day now. I hope I'm not coming down with something."

"Who needs whoops?" Sergei demanded, shaking his head toward Natalia, who turned a concerned face toward Jerry and picked up a box of tissues to offer him.

"We do!" the three boys replied.

Sergei sat back in his chair, knife and fork upright in his hand. "And you think you can operate a Bobcat?"

"Duh," Jake replied with a grin. "And even if we couldn't, Dana knows how."

Sergei's bushy eyebrows edged toward one another. "When would there be time for that? Levi and Jerry here had their first trail ride this afternoon, so they're probably bushed. And they're here for only four days, so I expect they want to fit in as much trail riding as possible, starting early tomorrow morning."

"We'll do it tonight!" Peter exclaimed. Jake and Levi nodded. Jake guessed that Dana would make the time to help them.

Sergei's knife and fork plunged back into his soufflé. "Natalia, should we let these boys use the Bobcat?

They think they can make a string of whoops and add to a jump all in one evening."

"*Da*, they are strong boys," she said, passing a loaf of fresh-baked bread toward Jake with a fond look, a bracelet dangling from her wrist. "Eat up for your energy," she added sternly, "but leave some for Dana, which boys can deliver please."

"Levi," Jerry instructed his son, "I'm okay with you helping the boys as long as you don't turn in too late."

An hour later, the three boys bent over the track with a shovel apiece as Dana sat at the controls of the Bobcat, scooping up massive amounts of soil and dumping it in strategic rows ready for the boys to finish shaping.

"Imagine how long it must've taken Sergei to build this whole track originally," Jake shouted over the Bobcat's motor as he slung some stones away and patted the earth with the back of his shovel.

"It would've taken ages. The guy must be a real motocross fanatic," Levi responded.

The three worked like dogs until they'd converted a small piece of a straightaway into a series of twenty whoops: hard-packed ripples. Then Peter took over the Bobcat to run loads of dirt to the top of two mini-mountains that formed a double jump. He got so into trying out all the tractor's controls and whipping up the slope faster each time that he nearly powered off the lip at one point.

"Stop being stupid!" Jake shouted, knowing Sergei would have freaked out if he'd seen that.

"Hey, no higher," Levi cautioned after another load.

"Yeah, that's enough," Dana agreed, one hand fishing a snack from her jeans pocket and the other leaning on her shovel. Jake was glad to see that she was being more careful about eating regularly. Sergei had said that hard work and sports could bring on insulin attacks. All four had sweated plenty reworking the track tonight. But it looked great.

"Hey, we really did create a whoops section in one evening," Jake enthused.

"Yeah, too bad it's getting too dark now to ride," Levi complained.

"It's definitely too dark, even with headlights on our bikes," Dana ruled. "Sergei would come out and chase us off."

"So what're we going to do?" Jake asked. "Play cards in our trailer? That'd be so boring." Everyone nodded their heads at that and fell quiet to think.

Jake looked around the darkening ranch. That's when he noticed Salt, Pepper, and Furball gathered at one end of their field to watch the goings-on. Their mouths worked back and forth as they chewed their cuds. They looked just like camels when they did that. Their eyes were on the boys and Dana, probably had been ever since the four had been working the track. They were highly curious animals, Jake had noticed. Way more intelligent-looking than horses. And he remembered that their feet allowed them to travel terrain that horses couldn't. "Hey Dana, ever taken the llamas on the motocross track?"

Dana paused from stomping down dirt on the top of the jump. She turned and grinned in the near-darkness. "Not that Sergei knows about."

"Yeah? Well, he'd hear our motorcycles out here, but he wouldn't hear the llamas."

The group went silent, watching the llamas, whose ears were pricked up as if they could secretly understand all that was being said, and were keen to run a moto.

"We could run them in the cart around everything but the big jumps," Dana said at length. "The llamas didn't get enough exercise today. Llamas actually have pretty good night vision. Way better than ours, for sure."

"Alright!" Jake pronounced, echoed by Peter and Levi.

Jake watched as Dana rounded up the llamas, popped harnesses over their noses, then backed them between the poles of the cart. The night air seemed to excite them; they tossed their heads about and pawed the earth.

"The cart won't fit more than three of us," Dana reminded them, "and I'm the only one trained to drive them."

"I'll watch during the first lap," Jake volunteered. He wished he had a night-vision camera. He couldn't wait to see how the llamas would negotiate the whoops, if Dana let them. Maybe he'd learn some motocross technique from them.

He felt only a little jealous as the cart took off, Peter whooping and hollering, Levi clutching the bar and grinning. Instantly they vanished into the night. Only the sound of the llamas' hooves battering the earth identified where they were. He wished the moon would shine more brightly so he could see them on the far side of the track. Dana had said she wouldn't take them up the jumps, but he tried to imagine the animals leaping a gap anyway. Like reindeer pulling Santa's sleigh. Reindeer with jacked-up back legs, rabbit ears, and soft, wet noses.

"Wheee!" he heard Peter shouting at the top of his lungs. Jake could feel the ground shaking as the team approached. But the team wasn't slowing; Dana was clearly going for another lap. He couldn't believe how fast they were going. Three llamas at 300 pounds each made for lots of animal muscle pulling the little cart and its excited passengers. As it thundered by, Jake couldn't tell which faces looked more excited: the llamas', or Peter's and Levi's.

His heart picked up as he heard the team approaching again. This time they were slowing.

"Whoa," Dana was saying, not loudly at all, as she pulled gently on the reins. "Attaboys. Easy, Furball."

The cart pulled up beside Jake as neatly as a bus at a bus stop. Levi piled out.

"Hey, Levi. You're the client. You don't need to get out," Jake protested.

Levi grinned. "Nah, Peter can have another go. I'm good."

Peter, sitting the far side of Dana, grinned at Jake. "Thanks, Levi!"

"Giddy-up!" Dana instructed her charges as soon as Jake was safely seated. They needed no encouragement, it seemed. Jake could swear they were going for a new speed record on this round. Wind cooled his face as he wrapped his knuckles around a small armrest at the side of his seat. The cart swayed and jolted as they traveled along the uneven ground. Could the llamas really see the ruts in the dark? Did they really know where they were going? Were they imagining themselves in a dead heat against other, invisible llama carts? They were picking up speed by the minute.

"I had no idea they could go so fast in the dark," he said to Dana.

"Neither did I," she said.

Jake glanced sideways at her, thought he saw a terse smile on her intent face in the dim light. He looked ahead, saw the newly formed whoops in deep shadow. *Lurch!* They hit the first one and started to leap. The cart went bang. No one needed to tell Jake the whoops were going to break the cart apart within seconds. He breathed a little easier when Dana yanked her reins to steer the llamas over to the ground beside the whoops.

Jake pictured himself as a Roman warrior riding in a gilded chariot. They doubled their speed on a banked curve heading to the straightaway. Any faster, and they surely risked overturning. Was Dana really letting her llamas go this speed or was she losing control? He turned to stare at her, saw a steely glint in her eyes: the look of a top-ranked motocross racer focused on winning her heat at any cost. Was she imagining a track full of racing chariots, too?

Jake dared not ask her to slow down; she'd laugh at him for days. Instead, he focused on the dim, shaggy rump of Furball in front of Dana. Furball, the devil, the berserk llama who'd been brought up isolated from fellow llamas. Furball, who'd be put down if he couldn't learn to work between Salt and Pepper. He and his partners seemed to be having the time of their lives on the motocross course.

Furball, Jake reflected, was a llama loner being handled by a human loner—a girl who'd been brought up isolated from fellow humans. Or so Dana's father had explained, according to Peter. Dana was like Furball: shy of her own species, a little berserk, but having the time of her life as she sped through the night sandwiched between two fellow motocross fans.

They were on the straightaway, nearing the double jump that Dana intended to veer around, when the llamas jerked their heads and hooves to the right and started up the dirt mountain. Had Dana's hand gone slack at the wrong split second, or was she crazed? The strong animals were pulling the cart right up the slope of a double-jump dirt pile! Jake's mouth dropped open, his heart pumped at double speed, and his hands tightened on the bar. The gap was forty feet. Dana had said llamas could jump maybe four. He turned to stare at Peter, whose face looked a little white in the moonlight. For an instant, he thought the cart's momentum was going to take them right up and over the lip. Then he heard Dana shouting and pulling on the lines. The cart plowed into the soft new dirt at the top, the way a semi-truck with failed brakes might use a sandy runaway lane off a mountain highway. With a lurch, the cart stopped dead as it became mired up to its hubs.

"Whoa, whoa, whoa," Dana was saying, her voice revealing an edge of panic. By the third "whoa," the llamas had stopped pulling. Their front hooves were inches from the edge of the jump, and they were trembling and pawing. Even though they were stopped, the situation didn't feel stable to Jake. The cart was now threatening to slide back downhill or tip. Not with me in it, he thought. He leapt out the same time Peter piled out the other side.

Jake threw a quizzical look at Dana as she murmured calming words to the shuffling llamas still on her reins.

"Can't …believe …they veered up here," she said, catching her breath. "I was steering them around it. But I imagined, just for a second, them jumping it. They must've read my mind and taken it as permission."

Jake and Peter stared at her. "Jake," she continued, "you and Peter get behind the cart and hold it while I unhitch them, okay? I'm not going to make them back this cart down a steep hill with loose dirt underfoot, especially in the dark."

Jake didn't like placing himself behind a half-stuck, tilting cart on a steep slope, but he and Peter did as they were told.

He watched as Dana freed Salt, then Pepper, then tried to hang onto the nose harnesses of both llamas to loosen Furball's lines. He heard her call to Peter for help, but the cart, no longer anchored in place by 900 pounds of llama, began to slide backwards.

"Push!" Jake yelled at Peter. He'd regret the timing of that shout later. Their shove pushed the front of the cart against the rump of the newly unleashed Furball, who promptly jerked free of his handler's grip, circled to the back of the cart, and emitted a deep rumble from his throat.

Jake looked up just in time to catch a volume of green spit in his left eye.

"Arghhh!" he cried as the slobber oozed down his face. He let go of the cart to wipe the slime away. With his one clear eye, he saw Peter leap to the right just in time to avoid wheel tracks on his body. As Jake tipped over into the loose dirt on the other side, one wheel ran over his ankles. He rolled over just in time to see Furball taking a flying leap down the back of the jump while veering away from the runaway cart. Jake reached out to clutch his ankle, relieved not to feel any pain.

"Oh, no!" Dana shouted.

The llama landed neat as a pro racer on the track and took off at high speed into the darkness, his reins dangling behind him. Meanwhile, the cart continued to roll backwards down the jump until it hit the track, bounced off two ruts, and came to a standstill. With its tangle of straps hanging from its upended front, it no longer resembled a golden chariot. And if Jake was a Roman soldier, he was a smelly, dirty, vanquished one now. He wasn't sure how long they all stood there, breathing hard, before a tall shadow with boots made its way up the hill and stood over him. Jake expected Sergei to lay into the whole group of them, especially Dana. Instead, the ranch owner bent down to inspect Jake's face, still plastered in green.

Sergei had Furball's leash firmly in hand. The source of the green guck stood placidly behind him, nose harness still in place. How had Sergei managed to catch that crazy Furball? Jake flinched as a second rumble sounded. But this time, it was the rumble of deep laughter, punctuated by a shaking belly, and a few high-pitched Russian words. Jake decided he definitely didn't want those words translated.

12   Upper Trail

Jake and Peter had meant to rise early enough to give the new whoops a try, but the two boys were still asleep when someone rapped on their trailer door.

"Hey Peter, hey Jake," came Levi's voice.

Jake shot up in bed. Guests weren't supposed to be up before junior guides. Sergei was going to be cross with them if Levi and his dad had eaten breakfast before the boys had risen and prepared the motorcycles for their morning ride.

"One second, Levi," he said, pushing his feet into Peter's sagging form above. "Peter," he hissed, "if Sergei's with Levi, we're in deep trouble."

Jake threw on his clothes and flung open the door. He breathed a sigh of relief when he saw Levi was by himself. "Sergei send you to fetch us?" Jake asked, looking toward the ranch house. "Sorry we're late.

We can be there in a minute."

"No hurry," Levi said, glancing around their trailer. "Can I come in?"

"Hey, Levi," Peter said groggily. "What's up? Ready for some awesome trail riding today? Let's find us some gnarly hills and crazy creeks, do some freestyle tricks."

Jake could imagine all the repairs that was going to require, but he was kind of hoping for some challenging stuff, too. He wondered what Sergei and Levi's dad would allow them to do.

"Good news," Levi said, stepping hesitantly into their trailer. "My dad's feeling lousy."

"That's good news?" Jake asked, smiling.

"I mean, he doesn't want to ride today. He's staying at the ranch house. So I asked if just us boys could go riding, with no Sergei along."

"And?" Peter demanded, sitting up and looking alert now.

"He said he was okay with Dana and us doing a day ride without him, as long as we promised not to be *gloopy*. What the heck is *gloopy*?" he asked, making a face at the boys.

Jake laughed. "That's Russian for silly. So he thinks we're trustworthy as long as Dana is along, does he? An all-guy trip would've been more fun."

"Maybe, but Dana's an awesome rider, and a

no-adults trip sounds like fun to me," Levi declared. "He said we can ride to the cabin and have our lunch there."

"Cool," Peter said.

"Yeah. This is a pretty sweet place. Llamas, trails, and a full racetrack. And tomorrow we do an overnight in the cabin, Sergei said. It has a fireplace and bunks and all? I'm sure Dad'll be fine by then."

"It'll be fun," Peter assured him, jumping down from his bunk. "So when do you want to leave for today's day-ride?"

"As soon as you and Dana are ready," Levi said, grinning. "By the way, Sergei told me to pour a bucket of cold water over you to wake you up."

"Not if you want us to show you the best places to ride!" Jake said, laughing.

By the time the two guides had shoveled bowls of corn flakes into themselves, suited up, and dragged the bikes out, Dana and Levi looked ready to go. Although it was not yet mid-morning, Jake could tell it was going to be a sweltering hot day. Good thing he'd checked the oil and coolant in all their bikes yesterday.

"Three guides to one ranch guest. Now that's service," Peter informed Levi as they buckled their fanny packs around their waists. "A freestyle maniac, a motocross expert, and a top-rated mechanic.

Between us, you've got everything covered."

"Hey," Jake objected, "I'm not just a mechanic." Peter's habit of dismissing his riding abilities was beginning to bug Jake big time.

"He's trying to flatter you so you'll keep doing his maintenance. He has no clue how to do it himself, 'cause you never make him," Dana said.

Jake said nothing, because it was true.

"I see, and I suppose you're all 'body and soul,' as Sergei says?" Peter asked Dana sarcastically. "I suppose you communicate with your bike, like you do with your llamas? Although that didn't exactly work out last night on the jump, did it?"

Dana pursed her lips and hopped in her saddle. "Better to communicate with my bike than not have a clue what it's made of," she retorted before kick-starting her bike.

Jake noticed Levi avoiding all their eyes as he stood beside his bike, hands hanging limply by his side. It wasn't professional to argue in front of a client, Jake knew. They were making Levi uncomfortable.

Dana pulled away first, heading toward the upper trail. That was fine with Jake. It had better stuff on it. It also had side trails he hadn't ridden yet that Dana could show them. Sergei usually stuck to the same well-groomed route.

Within half an hour, they were having a blast.

Sure enough, Dana was leading them on some side loops, where the four were forced to leap logs, splash through creek beds, and dodge around trees and boulders.

Soon, Jake figured they must be nearing the hideaway fuel-station treehouse. That was a good thing because he was getting nervous about running low on gas. Before they reached it, however, Dana drew up near some fencing. As her engine idled, she looked intently up and down the terrain. Jake paused beside her as Peter and Levi whizzed past. He could see no sign of the sheep or Hero, but that didn't worry him. Hero had lots of real estate.

"What's up?" he asked, aiming water from his water bottle down his throat.

Dana cut her motor and removed her helmet, as if listening for something. She didn't reply, which annoyed Jake.

"It's okay to answer a question now and then," he said.

"Shhh."

Jake listened. He heard birds twittering in the trees. He heard the breeze rustling leaves. He heard Levi's and Peter's now-distant motors revving it up. And maybe, just maybe, he heard sheep bleating from somewhere unseen. It all seemed peaceful and normal to him.

With no warning, however, Dana slammed her helmet back on her head and restarted her engine. She veered off the trail to travel the rough ground near the fence where it disappeared around a corner. Jake hesitated for a moment, then decided to follow her rather than catch up with the guys. The girl was on a crazy mission, for sure. She was leaping ruts, catching air, and ducking under branches that threatened to behead Jake behind her. He had to admire the way she handled the dried mud patches. He was having trouble keeping his bike upright on the dusty, cracked surface. Plus, his throat was getting drier and drier in the heat, and he was starting to fall behind. Where were Peter and Levi, anyway? The four were supposed to stick together.

As Jake labored up a steep incline, he felt his bike losing power. He downshifted fast, then put on a sudden burst of speed, only to nearly slam into Dana's empty bike on the far side of the rise. What the devil?

Dana had parked and was running down to the fence, where Hero was circling a tightly packed herd of sheep. Hero's long, spindly legs were running back and forth, back and forth, faster than Jake had ever seen Salt or Pepper maneuver.

"He's hyper. He looks like Sergei after three coffees," Jake tried to joke. He looked about, but there was no apparent danger. It was broad daylight, after all, and most sheep predators, with the exception of stray dogs, were nocturnal. Anyway, even if there was a threat, Hero clearly had it all under control.

Dana stood there, helmet in the crook of her arm. Her eyes were on Hero and his milling pack of charges.

"He's circling them like he has to get them all rounded up," Jake observed. "Guess he's doing a fire drill. Practise for when cougars are around here at dusk. Sergei says there are lots of cougars in this area."

Once again, Dana didn't reply. But slowly, her shoulders seemed to relax, and she twirled around and started back to her bike.

"Hel-lo," Jake said loudly as his boots walked across the dried mud. "I'm right behind you. In case you hadn't noticed, I followed you all the way here. Maybe we could stick together on our way back to finding the tour we're being paid to lead?"

Dana turned to look at him. Her face still held worry lines, although he couldn't imagine what for. "Sorry," she said. She hopped onto her seat and fired up the motor all in one move. Jake had to sprint back to his motorcycle to catch up with her once again. At least she was going slower this time, as if accommodating his jerkier, less confident riding. Soon Jake could hear Levi's and Peter's motors, which sent a flood of relief through him.

"Need gas!" he shouted at Dana as they powered up a hill and rejoined the trail. He thought she nodded, but wasn't sure. The two slowed as they sighted Peter. Oh no, Jake thought.

Peter was zooming up a smooth rock ramp. Barely into the air, he pushed on the handlebars to move the bike out in front of him. Quickly, he grabbed the rear subframe as he sailed through the air, stretched out behind the bike with only the one-hand point of contact.

"All he needs is a cape and tights to look like Superman," Jake said.

"A Superman Seat-Grab," Dana said beside him. "Impressive if he lands it."

If. Jake found himself clenching his teeth as the bike arced downward.

Even as Peter used his strong arms to pull the bike back under him, Jake had a feeling that Peter's timing was off, and this stunt was not going to end well.

Sure enough, as his motorcycle nose-dived toward earth, Jake watched Peter begin pulling, pulling, pulling up on his handlebars, as if they might unloose a reserve parachute. No such luck. His timing had been off from the start, and timing is everything in extreme sports. Jake drew in his breath as Peter's front tire hit hard. His body flew forward over the handlebars like a cowboy thrown from a rodeo bull that had stopped dead and lowered its head. Luckily for Peter, though, as the motorcycle did a headstand, he was thrown clear. Jake and Dana leapt forward as Levi stood there, his hand over his mouth.

13   The Lake

"You're okay but your bike is a mess," Jake ruled a few minutes later, after all three had inspected both rider and motorcycle. Jake wiped sweat off his forehead. It was midday and the sun had climbed high. It was baking him in his motocross gear.

"You call that okay?" Dana asked, pointing to the growing patch of dark blood on one of Peter's legs.

"It's fine. It'll stop in a minute," Peter said, wincing a little as he rolled his leggings up.

"It needs a washing," Dana ruled.

"Naaah," Peter insisted.

"Well, even if it needs a washing, we need all the water we have in our water bottles to drink, or we'll get dehydrated before we get to the cabin," Jake pointed out. "We also need to get to the refueling—"

"There's water just down this slope. A lake," Dana

informed them. "And I have to stop to check my insulin levels."

That produced a few seconds of silence, but in a way, Jake admired her for being straightforward with them.

"A lake? Hey, that'd be great. We could go for a swim, cool off while Jake fixes my bike," Peter suggested. "It's way too hot out here. Hey, where'd you two go, anyway? You're not supposed to take off like that."

Dana crossed her arms. "I had to check on Hero. Something was up over there."

"Yeah? Like what? I thought Hero took care of his own show," Peter said.

"Who's Hero?" Levi asked, bending over Jake as Jake fiddled with the bent gearshifter on Peter's bike.

"A llama who guards Sergei's sheep," Peter explained. "Now where's this lake? I could really, really use cold water on all these bruises."

Jake didn't doubt Peter had bruises. He was lucky if all he had were bruises and a leg wound. This freestyle stuff was going to cripple him. Jake didn't like it one bit.

Dana pointed to a nearby boulder the size of a house that jutted away from a drop. The boys moved cautiously onto it and peered over the side.

"It's tiny, but it'll do. Nice and close to this trail,

though a bit steep getting down there. Hey, how come you and Sergei have never pointed it out before?" Jake asked.

"It's not on public property," Dana said a little hesitantly.

"Yeah? So it's not Forest Service land?"

"No, it's part of the Bateman farm," Dana said, biting her lip.

"So we'd be trespassing. Well, they won't care. Especially if we explain we had to clean my wounds," Peter said.

"Thought you were fine and didn't need any first aid," Jake couldn't resist saying.

Peter made a face at him, all in fun. That showed he wasn't hurt too badly, Jake decided.

"You're sure it's okay to go into the lake?" Levi asked Dana.

She shrugged. Shrug No. 11, Jake thought to himself. She had too many shrugs for him to interpret. He wondered if the llamas had them figured out, and what Dana had thought was up with Hero a few minutes earlier.

"So how do we get down there with our bikes?" Levi asked.

Dana pointed to a narrow rut between two trees well to the left of the boulder. They piled onto their dirt bikes and revved their motors. All except Peter, who had to walk his. Jake hoped they'd be able to get it running again down there, or it'd be a steep push back up here. But a lake swim sounded pretty inviting to him. He'd swim before he tackled the stuck gearshift. Or maybe he'd refuse to fix it. Peter should have to do it. He was the one who'd messed it up by taking big chances, showing off for Levi.

They hung their fanny packs over their handlebars, all except Jake. He tucked his under Peter's motorcycle, ready for the repair work. They stripped to the shorts and T-shirts they were wearing under their motocross gear and dove in. Man, it felt good. Jake imagined his skin hissing like an overheated radiator getting a cool drink.

First, they did a couple of laps of the small lake to stretch their muscles. Then they crawled out at the far end and started doing fancy dives from a rock overhang. Levi discovered a rope swing hung from a tree, and they took turns playing Tarzan on that. It was while they were enjoying an all-out splashing war at the far end that the sound of a bike roaring to life jerked their heads up.

"Hey!" Peter shouted. "Someone's stealing our bikes!" He put his arms into motion and did a powerful American crawl across the short lake.

Jake, who was closest to shore, scrambled out and began running as a second bike fired up. He could see three kids, maybe nine, ten, and eleven years old. No way was he going to let them get away.

Now Levi and Dana were churning through the water like Olympic swimmers. Jake was nearly within reach of the third thief—Liam, the youngest of the Batemans. Jake could hardly believe the little squirt could get onto a 125. But the kid was heading for Dana's bike, which was set up for a pretty small person. Liam jumped on, toes barely touching the foot pegs. The boy started it and lurched out of reach just as Jake lunged to grab him around the waist. Jake fell. Sharp rocks pushed into Jake's bare knees and a mouthful of exhaust from Dana's bike set him off coughing. Peter limped past Jake, and soon all four teens were sprinting, barefoot, up the slope after the three bandits, who'd left only Peter's bike. By the time the guides and Levi had reached the main trail, however, all they could see was a cloud of dust lingering.

Jake, panting, shook his head. "This is a joke, right? This is their idea of a little fun? They'll come back in a minute, don't you think? They didn't even take the helmets."

Dana wiped perspiration from her forehead. "Can't count on it with the Bateman brats. They'll ditch the bikes eventually, 'cause they know we saw them. They won't sell them, I don't think. But I don't know if we'll get the bikes back today."

"The Bateman brats?" Levi spoke up. "As in the brothers who race 80s at all the motocross races? The ones with the scary-looking dad in his rusted-out pickup truck? Chuck, Ian, and Liam, their names are. The two older ones are too big for their 80s. Should be on 125s, really."

"That's them," Dana said, lowering herself onto a flat rock. "And they are on 125s now," she said bitterly.

"Then we can just go confront the dad," Levi suggested. "How far is their house from here?"

"It's not far, but I don't know if he'll help. He's not friendly. He gets his kids to steal stuff for him that he sells. There's no mom," Dana said with hunched shoulders and a pale face, not even looking at Levi. "What really sucks is they took my fanny pack. Does anyone have any food?" She stared at the pile of helmets on the ground and slumped further on the boulder. Jake realized she hadn't done her blood test before their swim. He felt his pulse quicken. Now she wasn't able to, and she wasn't looking good. How fast could her trouble come on? What should they do? He looked around frantically, saw that the Bateman boys had taken three of the four fanny packs: all but Jake's, which had been stowed under Peter's broken-down machine. Jake's pack had no food in it, only tools and a mini first-aid pouch.

"Hey!" Jake said, brightening. "They can't get far. They'll run out of gas soon. Or more like, they'll head straight for the treehouse as soon as they're forced to switch to their reserve tanks. We're really close to the treehouse. We can go hide in the bushes around it and catch them there!"

"But if they don't go there, or you miss them, or they've already drunk the juice in my pack, I'll be in trouble, Jake. It's more important to figure out how to get me some juice or food," Dana said in a tired voice. "How fast can you fix Peter's bike? Then someone can give me a ride to the cabin or back to the ranch. We're about halfway between the cabin and the ranch right now."

Jake leaned down to survey Dana's pale face. "Both the cabin and the ranch house are close to an hour's ride," he said in a grave tone of voice. "With two of us in the saddle, it'll take way longer than that. Plus, we'll have to stop for gas, and I don't know how long it'll take me to get this machine going again before we can do any of that." He glanced at the motorcycle, then turned to Peter and Levi. They were standing there, eyes darting from Dana to Jake as if waiting for orders.

"Peter, you grab two of these helmets and run to the treehouse and wait for the kids there. Get Dana's pack back even if you get nothing else. Levi, would you be willing to help us out?"

"Of course!" Levi said forcefully.

"Okay, Dana, tell Levi how to get to the Batemans' farmhouse. Levi, sprint over there and ask Mr. Bateman very nicely for some juice or food. I sure hope he's home. I'll get fixing this bike right away." He picked up his water bottle. "Dana, drink some water, get out of the sun, and relax the best way you can."

Dana nodded, accepted his water bottle, and moved under a tree. Peter, limping slightly, made it to the top of the rise leading to the trail, a helmet in each hand, and disappeared. Levi bent down in front of Dana and listened intently as she spoke while pointing to the far side of the lake. Then he was gone, moving with the grace of a long-distance runner.

Jake could feel a vein pounding in his neck. He could feel Dana's eyes on him as he opened his fanny pack and laid his tools out on the ground. He licked his parched lips, selected pliers, and jammed them under the bent gearshifter, pushing up gently. He pretended he was in the pits at a world championships motocross race and had only seconds to get the racer he served back onto his bike before that star lost any chance of securing the points he needed in the event.

"You're a pro wrencher. You can work under pressure," he told himself. "Dana's counting on you."

He leveraged the gearshifter free of the frame, trying to put it into neutral or first so he could start it. He tried starting it. His hopes rose as the bike rumbled and spit, but then it died. He tried again. Hand on the throttle, he coaxed it to life. He looked over, saw Dana's wan smile.

"Your limo, madam."

He could've left her there and motored off to catch up with Levi, but after the motocross race diabetic incident, he dared not leave her alone, even if he had no clue how to help her if she went into insulin shock. Anyway, she knew the way to the Batemans, and that had to be the nearest food source, as well as phone.

They donned the two remaining helmets and Dana climbed on. She clung to his belt with one hand and placed the other on the fender. Jake turned Peter's motorcycle around, followed the path along the lake, then sped up a stony hill in the direction he'd last seen Levi. It was awkward carrying an extra passenger on the little bike. But at least she was lightweight and knew when and how to lean with him. Jake was elated to see the rundown farmhouse within ten minutes' ride. Even happier to see Levi running toward him with a smile and a carton of orange juice. He was not so happy when he heard a gun fire and felt a bullet whiz over his head.

14   Stakeout

Jake hit the brake, cut the motor, and looked about. Levi had frozen mid-stride in the yard. Then a skinny, shirtless farmer with a grizzled face and filthy jeans emerged from his barn, rifle pointed at them.

No one moved as Martin Bateman approached. He had a menacing grin that gave Jake the sense that anything could happen.

"You're trespassing and stealing," the man accused in a raspy voice as he stopped a few rifle lengths away, gun trained on Levi. Jake noted several teeth missing.

"I—I tried knocking and calling out for you ..." Levi began, clutching the orange juice to his chest as if it might protect him from a stray bullet.

"Mr. Bateman," Jake addressed the man in a firm voice he hoped held no tremor, "Dana here is diabetic. She can go into shock if she goes too long without food. This is an emergency. We knew you'd be able to help."

The man glared at Jake and shifted the gun's aim to him. The pounding in Jake's ears picked up. He tried to breathe slowly. What was wrong with this guy? He was a father. Surely he understood. Silence held for half a minute before Jake noticed Martin Bateman glance sideways at Dana. Jake might have been imagining it, but he thought the farmer's leathery face lost a touch of its aggression.

Jake lifted his hands slowly from the stalled motorcycle's handlebars. "Mr. Bateman," he tried again, feeling Dana's sweaty, limp hands through the shirt on his back. "All we wanted was some orange juice for Dana here. Otherwise, she's going to faint. She's very ill."

"Faint" and "ill" weren't the right words, but Jake couldn't be sure the rifleman knew or cared what "diabetic" meant. The gun lowered, and the grizzled face turned toward Levi.

"Give it to her then," he snarled.

Levi, eyes bugged out, walked over to Jake, shuffling sideways like a crab as if fearful that losing sight of the farmer might change the man's mind. He handed the carton to Dana, eyes never leaving the gun. Jake, still straddling the motorcycle, heard the gurgle of Dana drinking the orange juice. It made his own throat feel sandpaper-dry.

"Thank you very much, Mr. Bateman," Jake continued, wondering where he was getting the nerve to communicate politely with a crazed gunman. "That's all we came for. We're sorry to have frightened you. We're very sorry. May we leave now?" He'd have liked to ask for a phone. He'd have liked to top up his water bottle in the Batemans' kitchen. He'd have liked to ask if the man could give Dana and Levi a ride back to the ranch. But he figured none of that was going to happen. Getting out of here without any more bullets ringing in his ears was his only goal.

The rifle lowered. "Get outta here!"

They needed no further encouragement. Jake kicked the starter and said a silent "thank you" as it caught. Levi ran alongside the motorcycle. Jake went slow and easy to make sure Levi could keep up. He had a feeling Levi was on the verge of freaking, that he might panic if Jake and Dana sped as much as a foot ahead. He wasn't sure if it was the midday sun or the rifle's aim on his back, but sweat seemed to pour off his neck as he put distance between himself and the farmhouse. Dana hadn't said a word, and he hadn't turned to check her out since they'd left the lake. He could feel her small hands clinging to his shirt. He had to trust that the juice was doing its job.

As the party of three burst over the rim of the hill, out of Martin Bateman's sight and range, Jake stopped and dismounted. He took a quick look at Dana. She smiled and gave him a thumbs-up.

"Thanks, Jake. That guy is scary."

"You've got that right," Jake said, relieved that she was looking like herself again. But his next priority was getting her fanny pack back and filling up the gas tank on this bike.

"Levi, this bike can't handle three," he said, noting that Levi's face had relaxed a little. "But Dana knows where the treehouse is. She'll direct you. Take over from me. I'll jog."

He pulled his helmet off and handed it to Levi. Levi nodded, donned it, and slid into the saddle as fast as Jake had slid off it.

"May the best racer win," Dana joked.

Hey, if she's joking, she's okay, Jake thought. He jumped back a little as Levi gunned the motorcycle. The boy took off along the lake's edge toward the main trail. Dana lifted her hand to wave goodbye. Jake started walking, then let himself look quickly over his shoulder toward the rise. No farmer with gun. He exhaled slowly to steady his nerves, then broke into a run. *Whew*. One crisis over. What next? And how fast could he run in motocross boots? Oh well. Peter had just run to the treehouse in his boots, with one slightly maimed leg. Who knew what Peter was up against this very minute with three young but tough Batemans? Now Jake knew where they got their tough-guy personalities. Some father. Peter, Jake decided, needed backup. Jake started to run faster.

Luckily for Jake, it wasn't far. He arrived to find Peter helping Levi hide the bike in some bushes while Dana scouted the trail in both directions.

"Good work, wrencher," Peter said. "Any idea how much I appreciate it?"

"Yeah right," Jake joked. "Shall we hide up in the treehouse?" He located the ladder in the bushes and leaned it up against the tree.

"Sure," Peter agreed. "There might be just enough room for both of us to squeeze behind the camouflage screen with the gas jugs. Dana, Levi, stow the ladder as soon we're up, okay?"

"Okay, then we'll go hide in the trees," Levi replied. The glow on his face made Jake decide Levi had gotten over the earlier scare and was having fun playing cops and robbers with kids.

"If no one comes within half an hour, we'll assume they've stashed the bikes somewhere or were stupid enough to have run out of gas. Then I'll take Dana back to the ranch," Jake said as he reached the platform right behind Peter.

"Those Batemans won't run out of gas," Levi said

as he maneuvered the ladder away and hid it in the bushes.

"Listen. They're coming," Dana said. She and Levi moved behind some trees. Sure enough, the whine of bikes was approaching from the cabin side of the trail. Jake and Peter crouched together behind the screen, all but falling off the far edge of the platform. The whiff of gasoline reached into Jake's nostrils.

As he peeked around the edge of the screen, he saw Hero down in his field. He wondered why Hero had rounded up the sheep earlier. I bet those Bateman boys were teasing them through the fence. Well, Sergei had said llamas remember who's family and who isn't. Those boys were going to get a swift llama kick some day for trespassing on Sergei's land. And wait till Sergei heard about the boys stealing their bikes. Then again, Jake's group had been trespassing on the Batemans' land. Sergei wouldn't think much of that.

Below him, the boys had cut their motors. The oldest two, Chuck and Ian, climbed off first. Jake couldn't help thinking both of them looked way more comfortable on the stolen 125s than they did on their own 80s back at the moto. Too bad their dad hadn't upgraded them. Jake watched as Chuck poked around the bushes, looking for the ladder.

"Help me lift this," Chuck ordered Ian, the middle

boy, when he found it. "Liam, you stand guard."

The littlest one crossed his arms and looked like he was going to object, but he moved up the trail and looked up and down it as he'd been ordered. It was the same boy, of course, who'd asked Jake to borrow his wrench at the race. And the same one he'd almost nabbed at the lake. Cute kid, Jake reflected, if you didn't know anything about his family. Jake wondered whether he'd ever have seen his wrench again if he'd loaned it to Liam at the race. He found himself feeling sorry for the boy.

Jake felt Peter lean toward him. "When I say 'go,'" he whispered.

Jake nodded. He was totally ready to leap on the first one up the ladder, but he worried about the other two brothers getting away. Still, Chuck might need two to pin him down. Levi could handle Ian, no problem. And Dana could probably hardly wait to get her hands on that little Liam.

The platform creaked as the biggest Bateman reached the top of the ladder, pressed the palms of his hands on the boards, and lifted himself up. Jake and Peter waited, holding their breath in the darkness of their "tent." Chuck took one step, two steps toward the camouflage screen. His hand reached in. Peter's hand met it and locked around his wrist.

"Go, Jake!" Peter urged.

The boy cried out and tried to wrench his arm away from Peter, but Jake lunged out of the hideaway and wrapped his arms around the thief's ankles. Chuck fell heavily to the platform, kicking and shouting warnings to his brothers. He used his free arm to land bruising punches first on Jake, then on Peter. His fist connected hard with Jake's jaw, but not enough to make Jake let go. Soon, both Jake and Peter were sitting on their flailing assailant. Beneath them, Levi had his arm around his victim's throat. And whatever Dana had said to Liam had made the little boy sit down and stare at the dust, looking dejected.

"Think you can steal our bikes, do you?" Peter began.

"You were on our property!" Chuck shouted from underneath them, still squirming.

"And you were on ours before that, harassing the sheep," Dana spoke up.

"Were not," Ian argued, trying to resist Levi's strong hold.

"Were," Dana replied confidently.

"Never saw us, got no proof," he said, eyes flashing at Levi, who looked to Jake like he was altogether enjoying this.

"Want to repeat that to the guard llama after we lift you over his fence and let him tell his side of the story?" Dana asked. "I should tell you that he has an excellent memory and a kick capable of killing a cougar." Jake couldn't believe she'd said that. He was trying to muffle a smile and noticed Peter doing the same.

"No," Ian said quietly, shooting a glance down the hill toward Hero. He stopped trying to pull away from Levi.

"So," Jake said. "You messed with our sheep and stole not only our bikes, but Dana's medicine." He gestured to the fanny pack that Dana was unbuckling from Liam's waist that very minute. Liam lifted his eyes and stared at Dana. "And you've stolen gas from here before. All we did was swim in your lake and get some orange juice off your dad."

"Orange juice from our dad?" Liam echoed with a stumped look.

"We went to your house for orange juice to keep Dana from dying, because you'd taken her medicine, which created an emergency," Jake declared, noting the look of concern and guilt that crossed Liam's face at that. All three brothers turned to stare at Dana as she lifted her blood-testing kit from the pack. She jabbed her finger with a needle on the end of something that looked like a pen. Then she dropped it onto a strip she fed into a calculator-sized machine.

"So your little joyride could've turned into a

murder rap," Jake carried on, enjoying the drama of the moment.

No one replied.

"So you owe us big time," he continued.

The oldest boy said nothing, just crossed his arms and turned distrusting eyes to Jake as Jake released his hold on him.

"We'll think about how you can repay us. Meanwhile, no one needs to report any of this to any adults. What do you think of that?" Jake concluded.

Chuck sat up and shrugged, then moved away from Jake and Peter.

"Whatever," he finally said, one eye wandering down to Dana popping glucose tablets into her mouth. "And you didn't say anything to our dad about the bikes?"

"Nope. And we're not going to. 'Cause you're going to repay us with a favor we decide on later. Agreed?"

The boy nodded slowly and looked at the ladder as if he wanted to be down it and away from there as fast as possible.

"Good. Then scram, 'cause we're late for lunch," Jake said.

Chuck scrambled down the ladder and took off, his brothers at his heels.

"And get yourself some 125s of your own. You're too big for 80s," Peter called after Chuck and Ian.

Now Jake and Peter looked at each other.

"Nice going, old buddy," Peter said.

"Yeah," Levi and Dana said together.

Jake smiled and grabbed the nearest gas container, looped the rope around it the way he'd seen Sergei do, and lowered it to the ground. He turned to his buddy.

"So, Peter, you're the gas station attendant here. Fill 'em up, sir. Don't spill a drop. Then don't forget to switch the reserve gas-tank levers to the off position, since we'll be back to running off the main tanks again."

"Yeah, yeah, yeah," Peter muttered, but he didn't argue.

15   Lower Trail

The alarm clock that Sergei had supplied the boys went off extra loud the next morning. Peter groaned and slammed it off. He was stiff and sore from yesterday's ride and fall. He wanted to fall back asleep. But he was a junior guide and today was going to be a big day: their first overnight trip to the hut with clients, following a warm-up ride in the morning. He opened an eye and peered out the trailer's window.

"Blue sky," he noted.

"Pretty much always blue sky here," Jake's sleepy voice responded from below him.

"Hope it's not as blazing hot as yesterday."

"It was pretty hot. But yesterday was fun," Jake said.

"Fun? What're you talking about? Staking out the kids? My bike accident? Nearly getting shot? Or watching Dana almost go into a fit? Pretty sketchy day all-around if you ask me. And my body feels like it's been run over by a truck."

"You're lucky you didn't get worse injuries, Peter. You ask for trouble when you do freestyle. Don't try tricks like that on the trail today or Sergei'll string you up. We're just lucky he knows nothing about what really went down yesterday. He thinks we had a fun day of biking out to the cabin and back."

"Well, we did get to the cabin and back," Peter said. "And Levi reported that we were excellent guides and all went well. What else would Sergei need to know? Best part of the day was that lunch Natalia left. I hear she's cooked us a great supper that Dana is delivering all the way to the cabin by llama cart this afternoon."

"Yes, but she's riding dirt bikes with us on the lower trail this morning," Jake reminded him. "Sergei says we ride to the lower trail's midpoint, have a picnic lunch, then come back here for a rest."

"Yup," Peter confirmed. "Then we pack up for the big ride that's supposed to start at five o'clock. We do the whole stretch to the cabin on the upper trail. Should get there just in time to put supper on by sunset. I think it's lame how Sergei advertises it as 'the sunset supper' in the brochures, but whatever. We're supposed to eat supper as the sun sets with all those views out the A-frame's windows. Not to mention hot cocoa and roasting marshmallows and popping popcorn in the cabin's big fireplace after sunset."

"All you think about is food," Jake said. "Speaking of which, it's your turn to make breakfast. And I'm not referring to Cocoa Puffs."

Peter sat up, swung his legs over the edge of the bunk, and jumped down to the trailer's cold floor. He pulled open a cupboard door and yanked out some pancake mix, a bowl, and a frying pan. "Just add water," he read from the package. "I can handle that." He'd show Jake he could cook a real breakfast. Although the truth was, Peter liked it much better when Jake was on breakfast duty.

An hour later, happily stuffed with warm pancakes, the boys had all six bikes ready to roll. Like Sergei, Levi, and Levi's dad, they'd also delivered their sleeping bags and overnight gear to Dana. She was packing these into the llama cart nearby, ready for delivery with Natalia's supper later that afternoon.

"Guess the llamas aren't going to go very fast with that load," Peter said, watching her strap the bags down.

"Nope, but coming back in the evening, we'll have no load, and we'll fly," she said mischievously.

"Weather report says forty percent chance of rain. Doesn't look like it's going to happen," Peter said, double-checking that the wide blue sky was still there.

"Let's hope not. Llamas hate rain," Dana said.

"So do motorbikes," Peter replied, flashing back to the mud bath the Spokane course had turned into last week.

"Guides!" Sergei called from the house. "All set? Levi and Jerry here are itching to go."

"The lower trail isn't as fun as the upper trail," Peter informed Levi as they headed off, riding abreast on its wide, dusty start. "But you can see all the way to Idaho from there. Just wild countryside, no houses. Perfect country for dirt-bike riding. If we had permission, we could build trails up here for years and never run out of backcountry."

"Cool. Guess that's why it's called Back-of-Beyond Ranch."

"Yup. Race you to the creek."

Levi, Peter had noticed, needed no encouragement to go for it. The two took off on a pretend "enduro," or long-distance race. They roared past Sergei and Jerry, who were riding slowly to chat with each other. Really, Peter knew, Sergei was going lazily to accommodate the nervous riding of Jerry. As the boys passed, the men smiled, and revved up to join the race for a few minutes. Then they eased back, riding just behind Jake and Dana. As for Jake and

Dana, Peter and Levi served them up a whirlwind of dust.

Peter half expected Jake and Dana to speed up. He kind of wanted to race Dana. But Dana stayed back, didn't seem to be in the mood. And Jake probably didn't want to take any chances of hurting his bike, the wuss. Or maybe those two were saving their energy for the afternoon.

Once he and Levi were well ahead of the others, Peter started doing more whips and jumps. He loved the sensation of flying on his bike. It made him feel so free. Up and down the gentle rises he went, Levi on his tail or alongside. Anyone watching them would have had to pause to admire the well-choreographed ballet of wheelies over the whoops, the way they took the fast line on the corners, and the way they used everything on the trail to get the bikes airborne.

Levi was a great biker, Peter had to admit. That made him fun to ride with. He made everything look easy: the dirt-bank-hugging turns, the slalom action around stones, and the casual no-handers on small jumps. They even paused once to do trials riding: jumping their bikes from object to object without touching their boots down for balance. As they neared the creek, they were riding abreast, as if happy to declare their race a tie. Their bikes halted on the edge of the creek as decisively as horses bent on lowering their heads into it for a drink. They lifted themselves off their saddles and squatted down to splash the cool, sparkling water over their faces.

"Sure feels good in this heat," Levi observed, lifting his head to take in the scenery around them.

"I love this place," Peter replied. "We should probably hold up here for the slow-pokes."

"Okay. How far are we from the lunch spot?"

"Close."

"No view from here, though."

They took turns tossing pebbles over the creek until they heard the motors of the others approaching.

"Everything okay with you two?" Sergei called out as he pulled up.

"You betcha," Peter responded.

"Levi," Dana spoke up as she drank from her water bottle. "You know we go single file on this next stretch and keep it slow?"

"Yup. So we're coming up to the place with the cliff and view?"

"Correct," Jake replied as he lifted his goggles and bent down to splash water on his face.

Sergei, who'd been idling, let his bike lurch forward into the creek without warning, then accelerated. Clearly, Peter realized, he was determined to place himself in the lead before Peter or Levi could kick-start their bikes. Peter fell into third place behind

Jerry, who seemed to like keeping just behind the Russian. Shortly after they'd all motored across the shallow stream, the ground to their left began to rise steeply, while a bank to their right fell away abruptly. Somewhere fifty vertical feet below wound a river into which the creek they'd just crossed spilled.

Peter looked to his right; it made his fingers tingle and his body stiffen. Definitely not a place you'd want to speed or slip in the dirt. And yet … He pictured a daredevil accelerating his motorcycle off the edge, then letting go of his handlebars, pulling a parachute, and floating gently to river's edge at the bottom of the gully. Freestyle legend Travis Pastrana did something like that in the Grand Canyon in 2001. Of course, Pastrana could afford to write off motorcycles if anything went wrong. Peter needed a sponsor before he got into anything too wacky.

Lifting his head to the right, Peter drew in a slow breath. Such a view up here: rounded hills marched away like shadows of one another as far as he could see. Just then, his front tire hit a small rock, shooting it off the trail and down into the river gully. Peter pulled his eyes back straight ahead. He relaxed a little as he saw the trail widening up ahead.

"Yeah!" Peter shouted as a treehouse with camouflage screen came into sight a short while later. "Lunch!"

Like its twin on the upper trail, the refueling station was located roughly halfway between the ranch house and cabin. Peter's stomach rumbled as the noonday sun reflected off a bright canister. That had to be the picnic lunch Natalia had fixed for them, which Dana had dropped off earlier in a container safe from small animals.

Peter watched Sergei dismount and prop the ladder up against the tree.

"Levi and I will help," he offered. "This treehouse has way better views than the upper trail's."

Sergei stood back to let the boys clamber up and fetch the canister. "To your left, Hero and his ladies," Peter told Levi, gesturing at the sheep field. "To your right, Idaho."

"Cool," Levi said, eyes on the sparsely treed hills. "Quite the view. You could rent this treehouse to landscape artists."

"Now there's a thought!" Sergei said, laughing. "Rope down those gas containers while you're up there, boys."

Peter clambered down with the lunch container and pulled open the top. He remembered to pass it to Jerry and Levi first.

"Whoa, look at the size of these sandwiches," Jerry said appreciatively.

"This is my kind of refueling station," Peter

agreed as the triple-decker, turkey-bacon-cheese sandwiches on home-made bread, apples, and muffins came around.

"Peter needs regular refueling," Jake teased. "He has a very inefficient engine."

"Or maybe I do more miles," Peter retorted with a smile.

First they filled themselves up on Natalia's delicious sandwiches, then they topped up the gas in the bikes.

Then, all too soon, it was time to head back to the ranch. Once again, Peter rode close to Levi, playing off every feature of the trail they could find. This time, Jake and Dana joined in the exuberant riding, the foursome leapfrogging past one another all the way back to the ranch. He was tired as the group pulled up to the railing around the ranch house's wraparound porch.

"Rest up, gang," Sergei suggested as they cut their motors and Natalia, in a short cotton dress and glittery sandals, appeared in the doorway. She held a tray of iced tea, fresh-baked chocolate chip cookies, and some small sandwiches. Placing the tray on a wicker table beside two wicker easy chairs, she smiled toward Levi and his dad. Peter's tongue licked his lips as his weary eyes focused on one of the glasses of iced tea. The ice cubes sparkled and danced between the lemon wedge and straw. But he counted only two glasses: for Levi and his dad.

"Jake, Peter, see you at five o'clock sharp," Sergei dismissed them. "It's one o'clock now. Rest up till then."

Peter sighed and turned to Jake. As Jake removed his goggles, Peter laughed at the raccoon-style "mask" that the morning's dust had left around them.

"To our wee castle, then," Peter said, "for a wee nap."

"After you wash down the bikes," Dana reminded them as she let herself into the llama enclosure to feed and water her charges.

"That girl has lost her shyness with us *too* fast," Peter grumbled to Jake.

16   Losing Sergei

"**S**ure the llamas can handle that load?"
Jake asked Dana as she was harnessing the llama team
to the piled-high cart a few hours later. She'd managed to fit the entire group's sleeping bags, packs, and
supper containers onto the seat beside her. Straps
shaped the pile into a tidy tower. The outfit reminded
him of the lopsided sleigh in Dr. Seuss's children's
cartoon, *How the Grinch Stole Christmas.*

She delivered her reply with a sardonic smile. "Are
you insulting my team or my packing skills?"

"Sorry. Guess you know what you're doing," he
apologized as he strapped his fanny pack around his
waist. He watched Sergei emerge from the barn with
three more fanny packs dangling from his fist. Sergei
tossed Peter's to him and lay one in the cart's driver's
seat. He loosened the straps of the last one to buckle
it around his paunch. Then he donned his motorcycle

helmet, winked, and took a flying leap onto his bike from behind, kick-starting it as he landed.

"Like an American cowboy, *da*?" he asked with a triumphant grin.

"Sure, Sergei, all you need is a lasso," Jake suggested.

The rumble of four more bikes starting up filled the air as Natalia, between touching up her makeup, waved goodbye from the porch. Dana, absorbed with double-checking the llamas' harnesses, raised a hand as well.

Even though the motorcycles could go more than double the cart's speed, Jake guessed Dana would have finished her delivery by the time the bikers pulled up at the cabin. That's because the bikers would take plenty of side trips off the main trail and pause to refuel. Dana, on the other hand, would be bent on as quick a round trip as she could, both to give the llamas a vigorous workout and to return to the ranch before it became dark around nine.

In a way, he wished she was riding with them this afternoon. Peter and Levi were biking way too fast and aggressively for him to want to keep up, and Jerry and Sergei seemed to have formed their own pairing. Jerry, in fact, was boring. He rode slowly and pensively, as cautious as a learner. Jake felt like the odd one out. Still, it was nice to be out in the fresh air again, and he was looking forward to the overnight at the cabin. As his bike motored along the well-worn upper trail between the other boys and the men, he glanced at the late afternoon sky. All blue still, except for a distant black blotch like an ink stain to the east. He reminded himself to keep an eye on that blob, though he figured Sergei had taken note of it, too.

As trees whizzed by and ruts occasionally challenged his tires, Jake kept trying to guess where Dana was on her trail. When Peter and Levi veered onto the second side trip of the day and began catching air every few minutes, Jake tried to mask his jealousy by picturing Hero lifting his head as the llama cart rolled by. He checked his watch. Yeah, Dana would be about halfway by now and looking forward to getting rid of that load so she could race home. This morning she'd commented proudly on how far Furball had come.

"He's calmed down enough that we might be able to sell him and take on another," she'd told him.

"Won't you miss him?" Jake had asked. He'd felt stupid the minute he'd said it. She was a farmer's kid and a ranch hand. Her job was to retrain berserk llamas and sell them so she could take on more, not adopt them as pets. Furball was her first "client," her proving ground under Sergei's watchful eye. But instead of laughing at Jake, she'd taken the time to explain all that patiently. Jake could swear she was getting less shy with Peter and him at the same rate Furball was getting more cooperative in his harness.

Jake shifted into a higher gear with thoughts of catching up to Peter and Levi. As he approached, he admired the way the pink of the oncoming sunset shone through the clouds of dust they were creating. The dust rendered the sun psychedelic shades of orange and rose. It reminded him of the way colored spotlights highlight the special-effect clouds that frame rock bands on a stage. For a moment, the entire trail seemed to be a palette of colors: the orangey hues of the sunset, the blue of the sky, the green of the trees, the brown of the dry trail. But wait. Another color seemed to be bullying its way onto the canvas, slowly but surely aiming to dominate. Jake's head swiveled to the east. The thunderhead. The little ink spot had turned into an industrial-sized spill. The gentle summer breeze had developed a sudden chill to it.

Rain itself wouldn't be that big a deal, Jake knew. Dirt bikers never cancel a trip for a little rain. In fact, riding in mud is a skill every motocross racer has to learn at some point. But Jake felt his spine shiver as he examined the clouds again. This was going to be a big one, and it was going to make the evening light disappear long before its normal time. Although they'd been out for more than an hour already, they weren't even to the treehouse yet. Sergei and Jerry had seemed content to let Peter and Levi take every single side trail on the upper section, and Jake had been following along with his mind anywhere but on the trip. Jake glanced at his fuel gauge. Whoa. Good thing they were close to the treehouse.

"Jake!" Sergei's shout surprised Jake as the rancher pulled up beside him. Jake had been so zoned out, he'd thought Sergei and Jerry were in front of him. Sergei pointed to his fuel gauge.

Jake nodded vigorously. "Yup, straight to the treehouse," he suggested.

He found himself between the two men as they sped up and signaled to Peter and Levi. Jake watched Peter glance down to his fuel gauge. He hadn't been checking either, Jake guessed. In fact, as Jake peered closer, he realized that both Peter and Levi were on their reserve tanks. Cutting it pretty tight.

Within minutes, Peter's bike began chugging and snorting, then jerked to a stop. "I guess running on fumes doesn't last forever," Peter shouted with a playful grin at Jake as he pointed downhill to the treehouse. "What timing, eh?"

"Lucky," Jake remarked dryly as Peter rolled his silent bike downhill and Levi's bike started coughing. Jake and the men, having biked more slowly and less aggressively, still had a little in their tanks.

As Jake scrambled up the ladder, he heard Sergei curse loudly, then apologize. Jake peered down and saw him staring at his unzipped fanny pack, his forehead wrinkled with concern.

"Forget something?" Jake asked.

"I picked up Dana's instead of mine," Sergei said, eyes rising to meet Jake's.

"So she must have yours," Peter chirped cheerfully. "Told you our packs looked too much alike." Then he went silent as the seriousness of the situation sank in for the three guides.

"What's the big deal?" Jerry asked, fidgeting as he picked up on the guides' somber looks.

"Dana needs her pack for some medicine," Sergei said, speaking slowly as if to cover a rising panic.

"Oh. Guess that means you change packs with her at the cabin?" Jerry suggested, eyebrows raised.

This made Sergei's head jerk up toward the sky. Had he only just noticed how their blue bowl had turned very black? He turned to look at Jake and Peter.

"Dana will have delivered her load to the cabin by now, and she'll be racing back to beat the rain and get to her medicine supplies back at the ranch house. The llamas don't like rain, and they don't keep their footing well in mud."

"So with no medicine on her, she won't take the chance of waiting around at the cabin for us," Peter finished for him.

Sergei nodded stonily and zipped up Dana's pack. He looked to Jake and Peter with such heavy features that Jake had the impression he was begging their forgiveness for mixing up the packs.

"She's alone," Jake heard himself saying. He knew that for Dana, not being able to test herself was a big deal. His own palms were sweating at the notion of what could happen. He turned as Sergei studied his watch, then fired up his motorcycle.

"Jerry, Levi, I'm sorry but I have to deliver this pack to Dana. You're in good hands with Jake and Peter, and I'll be back so fast you'll hardly miss me."

"But what if you miss her?" Peter blurted out.

"No chance of it. I'm going to cut through the sheep field," Sergei said as he revved his engine. "She can't have reached the lower trail's refueling station yet. I'm sure to catch her between there and the cabin if I leave now and hang a left at the lower trail."

"Go for it," Jake urged him before Peter could say anything.

"Dana is diabetic," Levi explained to his father, who nodded soberly. "She used to go to my school."

Jerry kept nodding, then straightened up. He squinted at the sky and frowned. "Well, Jake and

Peter. Levi says you know the trail from here to the cabin well, so lead on. I do believe we're going to get poured on before we reach it."

17   Rain

Jake didn't mind that Sergei had left Peter and him in charge. That's what junior guides were for, right? It made him feel proud and important. Anyway, not only would Sergei be back very shortly, but their clients were competent bikers. Well, okay, Jerry was a little jittery, but he was still competent, and Levi was totally okay. So there seemed nothing to worry about, unless it was the disappearing light and the oncoming rain. But there was still just enough time to get to the cabin by nightfall, and biking in the rain was no big deal. Heck, where Jake came from—just northeast of Seattle in British Columbia—it rained all the time. If you waited only for sunny days to ride, you'd hardly ever ride.

But when the black clouds overhead finished choking off any trace of blue, and fat raindrops began to fall, a sliver of worry entered his mind. Within minutes, he realized how this region differed from his home trails: rain here was so rare that the soil seemed unable to cope with a deluge. Instead of forming the odd puddle to splash through, or creating a harmless layer of mud, the rain and dust formed a slippery goo, a clay that acted like black ice on a highway.

All week, the group had been speeding over tracts of dried mud that held so many cracks, they often resembled a map depicting small countries' borders. Now, the cracks were capturing rivulets of water until they could hold no more. That's when entire countries seemed to rise up in revolt and slide across borders. Some cracked into smaller pieces, like blisters popping. Others appeared to lose their moorings, lurching forward like floating islands with the pressure of a passing tire. Slippery wasn't the word for the fast-changing trail; it was like a minefield of unpredictable surprises growing muckier by the minute.

Streamlets of brown water appeared from nowhere on the slope to their left, and charged down like armies to puddle on the trail.

Everyone slowed after Peter fishtailed so badly he nearly went down. They slowed even more after Levi, while taking a banked turn in slow motion, spun out and did a full face plant.

"Hey, some women pay big money for mud facials," Peter kidded him.

"Yeah, when they could just take up dirt biking in the rain," Levi spluttered back.

"Please be more careful, son," Jerry spoke up, the worry lines on his forehead showing whenever he paused and lifted his goggles.

Pretty soon, they were taking turns between second and third gears. But the slower they went, the faster the rain came and the further away the cabin seemed. Soon, trickles of water sliding down the hill joined forces into one massive waterfall, bringing with it small rocks that would roll down in front of their bikes on very little notice.

The trail was beginning to feel like a filling ditch, yet Jake could figure out nowhere else to ride. He'd cut his speed so much he was getting stuck every few minutes. Yet if he tried to go faster, he lacked the time to react to the rocks slithering onto the path from the bank on the left. Between the downpour and mud flicked up by the others, he was also having trouble seeing through his goggles.

He'd ridden in rain and mud plenty of times, but conditions were getting so serious, that he figured if this had been a motocross race, officials would be discussing shutting it down.

"Jake, Peter," Jerry shouted. "I wonder if we should pull over and wait this out or something. His voice held the edge of panic.

Jake threw a glance at Peter. If they could be certain that it would ease up soon, it made sense. He wished Sergei were here to help them make the decision. In fact, checking his watch, he realized with a panic that Sergei should have rejoined them long ago. All he'd had to do was run down through the sheep field and turn toward the cabin. By Jake's calculations, he'd have met Dana, exchanged packs with her, and motored right back up the hill just before the rain had started.

Something has gone wrong.

Jake motioned for all four bikers to come abreast of one another and let their motors idle. "Peter, I'm going to make sure that Sergei is okay," Jake finally declared, loudly enough for Levi and Jerry to hear. "I'll follow his tracks through the sheep field."

Peter stared at him. "But why wouldn't he be okay?"

"It's been too long."

Peter lowered his eyes to his mud-spattered watch and rubbed its face with the clean inside of his glove. His eyes took their time returning to Jake's face. "Okay. We'll be alright. You and Sergei can catch up to us at the cabin along the lower trail to avoid reclimbing that hill. See you at the cabin, then. That dinner is going to taste so good, and I'm really glad they have towels and showers ..."

Jake nodded. "Look after Peter, Levi," he joked.

"Absolutely," Levi returned with a smile, leaning back on his bike seat in a relaxed manner.

"You're sure you need to check on Sergei?" Jerry asked, eyes darting from Jake to Peter and back again.

"I am."

"Go on then. We'll be fine. Be careful in this muck." Jerry was trying hard to put on a brave face, which prompted Jake to reach out and pat him on the back.

"I will." Jake turned his bike around slowly and headed back to the treehouse. They hadn't really come all that far, but it seemed to take forever to get there as he dodged rocks newly embedded in the soupy trail. His shoulders relaxed a little as the refueling station came into sight. He looked down the slope and spotted an imprint of Sergei's bike tires. Only trouble was, Sergei had done his run before the rain, so like Hansel's and Gretel's bread crumbs, the ranchman's tracks were fast disappearing.

"Oh well," Jake thought, relaxing. "It's no big deal finding my way from here to the lower trail. Can't really go wrong cutting through Hero's field."

Of course, it meant sidehilling down to the fence, but they'd practised that. Even Eddie had almost managed to reach Hero's fence that day, so no need to be nervous. Okay, so it was way more slippery in the rain. But it was doable, Jake was sure.

Now, what is it Sergei had taught them about sidehilling? Something about keeping his speed low—he remembered Sergei making Eddie repeat that. Oh, and you use ruts and little terraces and try to keep traction. He peered over the edge of the hill. He couldn't see much in the way of ruts or terraces, but he took a deep breath and told himself he'd done it last time—most of the way, anyway—so he could do it this time.

"Well, here goes," he said.

He did a cursory check of possible lines, but uppermost on his mind was getting down this slope before it got any muddier. He also kept twisting his head to see if Hero was around. Would've been nice to have the llama there to greet and congratulate him when he arrived at the bottom. But there was no sign of the llama or his flock.

Jake started out okay. He kept his speed low and steady, and his wheels in line. "Where the front tire goes, the rear usually follows," he reminded himself. His mouth went a little dry as things got wetter and steeper. He swallowed hard as he traversed above a particularly steep place. Had this section been there the day they'd all sidehilled down? Must've been. He put more pressure on the outside foot peg.

"I'm doing okay," he tried to reassure himself, "but

the rain is seriously messing with this hill, and I wish it wasn't starting to get dark." Yikes! He looked ahead, suddenly clueless about where his "line" was. When he started to slip, he grabbed a handful of front brake. Not a good idea. Later, he remembered that he was supposed to avoid braking—that it was better to back off the throttle and try coasting to a stop. And if you did have to brake, it was best to use only the rear one. He knew that, but somehow the information was all jumbled inside his panicking brain. The horrifying sensation of sliding notified him that it was now too late. The outside edge of his knobby tires dug in the air, desperately searching for traction. He stood on his pegs, hands sweaty, throat tight. Wait! Sergei had said stay sitting to lower your center of gravity!

As he sat back down, the motorcycle beneath him began to skid faster down the almost vertical face. "No!" Jake knew he was hooched. He might have cried out—he couldn't remember later—as the heavy machine turned into a toboggan on a mud run. But he did do one thing right: he leaned into the hill as he went down—and down, and down. At some point, rider and bike hesitated on the top of an embedded boulder, then separated. Jake lay sprawled just above the rock, one boot hanging over the edge. The bike, having hit it heavily, made a scraping noise that made Jake wince.

He lay there for a few minutes, his back soaking up the mud like a sponge and his face collecting the sharp sting of raindrops. He opened his mouth and let the sky offer him a drink as he waited for stabs of pain to identify themselves. Gradually however, he decided the boulder's flat, muddy top had collected him like a hospital bed and spared him the peril of plunging over its unyielding surface like his bike had. He knew he was bruised. He sensed that was all.

After a few minutes, he made himself sit up. His wet, gloved hands massaged his sore left leg, whose bruises he imagined would be pretty colorful tomorrow. He concluded he was fine. In other words, lucky.

He crawled to one side of the boulder, then slid down the mud slope to where his bike lay sprawled. It looked for all the world like a horse that had thrown itself off a cliff.

"I'm sorry, I'm sorry," he muttered to it as his hands went to new dents in its gas tank, new scratches in the paint, bent handlebars, and twisted forks. He sighed at the sight of a tweaked front rim, as well. He tried to stand it up but had to ease it further down the final stretch of hill first. There, he unzipped his fanny pack, removed his helmet, and cursed the downpour, which only seemed to get heavier by the minute. Rummaging around for his tools, he set to work. Sweat and rain joined forces on his forehead and the darkening sky merged with his darkening mood. He tried straightening his handlebars and realigning his front forks. He wished he had a mallet to take the nasty tweak out of his front rim. He'd hit something so hard that he could see grass lodged between the rim and bead of the tire.

"It's hopeless," he finally told himself, shivering and looking back up the muddy slope.

All too late, Sergei's words returned to him: "Sidehilling is super tricky, and almost impossible in mud. Take lots of time to figure out the smoothest line …"

"Almost impossible in mud," Jake repeated, looking down and wiping gobs of it off his jersey. "Sergei got down here just in time, before the rain. I shouldn't have tried. And I sure didn't take time to figure out a line."

Jake stood and gave the bike a half-hearted kick. "Sorry," he apologized to it again. He hung his head. He didn't like to admit failure, but it was time to face up to the fact he could not fix this bike. Not here, not now. He turned his face upwards and let the cold rain spatter on it and drip off his chin. The dark branches of trees high above waved in the wind as if trying to get his attention. He squinted, then let his eye roam around the gray, sodden sky.

It was way too early for dusk, but rainstorms have a way of rushing nightfall. He examined the shadowy trees all around him and shivered. Until now, he'd been so bent on pursuing Sergei and Dana, then fixing his bike, that he hadn't been thinking about his own safety.

He scanned the wet terrain around him and tried to clear his mind. He was drenched, but if he kept moving, he'd stay warm enough. He figured he had two choices. He could walk back up the hill and traipse to the cabin on the upper trail. He'd be on his own till he got there, for sure, but he wouldn't get lost, and he had a tiny flashlight in his fanny pack. Or he could carry on following Sergei's tracks across the sheep field, hope to join up with the ranch owner on the lower trail, and get a ride on the back of his bike. The only danger, he thought as he cast another glance around, was wildlife. Specifically, cougars. This was their hunting time and their hunting range.

He decided to carry on through the field and go for the lower trail.

An image of cougars crouched in the growing shadows all around forced itself on him. He shivered and eyed his tool kit. His best weapon was a crescent wrench. He unzipped his pack and placed it firmly in his wet left hand. He pulled out his small tire iron with his right hand. Either tool would land a pretty damaging blow to the skull of a cougar interested in clamping its jaws around any part of his body. They almost always went for the back of the skull though, didn't they? He'd once heard that anything under 100 pounds was fair game to a cougar. And they liked surprise attacks, so if he kept looking around, he might discourage one.

I weigh more than 100 pounds, he reminded himself with gritted teeth. But do cougars stop and ask what you weigh first? He'd never given the cougars around here much thought before now. With a loud motorcycle between one's knees, it's not an issue. Both the noise and speed of dirt bikes offer an element of protection to a rider, not to mention that dirt bikers mostly ride in groups. Cougars, he'd read, are more likely to pounce on solo travelers or stragglers. Especially children.

Here he was standing on a wet hillside with nothing but a dead motorcycle beside him and a tool in each hand. He felt small and vulnerable. Cougars hunt at dusk and have very sharp night vision, he remembered. He clamped his helmet back on his head—for the warmth it gave, he told himself.

"Get going," he ordered himself. "It's getting darker by the minute."

18   Hero

He gave his motorcycle one last, sad look and turned to squish through the mud toward the field. There was no sign of Hero or the sheep, but that wasn't surprising. It was a big field.

He came to the low fence and found the gate Sergei had used. The fencing either side of the gate wasn't the kind that would stop Hero from jumping out or a cougar from jumping in; it was just to keep the sheep within boundaries. Since Hero would never leave his sheep, and since Hero's presence discouraged cougars from creeping up on the sheep, Sergei hadn't felt a need to go to the expense of putting in a tall fence.

The field made for mushy and uneven walking, and the motocross boots were already producing blisters on his heels and toes, but for some reason, Jake felt safer in the field. It was a false sense of safety, of course. A cougar bent on stalking him could still move through the woods just the other side of the fence and bide its time until ready to spring. Sergei had told them that cougars could leap twenty-five feet. That put Jake only two cougar bounds from the woods.

He quickened his pace and perked his ears for the sound of the llama cart or Sergei's motorcycle. Halfway across the field, he felt his heartbeat pick up and the hairs on the back of his neck prickle. Why? Had he heard something, or was he letting his imagination scare him?

He clutched his tools more tightly and turned slowly to study the closest section of woods. A dark patch of trees drew his eyes in and wouldn't let them go. He had heard something in there, a twig snap. He was sure of it. Although he could make out nothing, he was dead-certain that his eyes were locked with the eyes of something keeping itself hidden from view. Something with night-vision eyes. Something stalking him.

"I weigh 150 pounds!" he shouted to it, raising his arms and waving his tools. "And lots of that is muscle!"

Nothing but silence.

He moved forward again, quickening his pace, but threw ever more frequent glances that way. Once, he was sure—so very sure—he saw movement.

A slinking kind of movement that sent electrical impulses from his heart to his legs, inspiring them to move faster. He knew what you were supposed to do if you encountered a cougar in the wild. You were to face it, arms raised, with a defiant look, and back away slowly. Never, ever run or turn your back on it. But he couldn't very well back away across half a field without tripping and landing on his back in the mud. He had to be keeping an eye out for the fence that separated the field from the lower trail. He had to keep following Sergei's tire tracks, and watching for Sergei. Anyway, he chided himself, he might be making it all up.

He decided to sing, even if his slightly trembling voice caught now and again. He racked his brain for the lyrics to heavy metal songs because cougars surely wouldn't like those. When it came time for an aggressive drumbeat in the song, he used his wrench and tire iron to air-drum.

He kept walking beside what he could see of Sergei's tire tracks, head turning so often to the woods that whatever was in there must think his head was stuck in a peculiar sideways position. Lower trail, where are you? Sergei, Sergei, Sergei, please be there. Then he saw them: the fence, the trail, the treehouse, and Sergei's parked motorcycle! Without thinking, he started to run. He heard the squish, squish of his boots in the mud. The ground seemed to pound with his sprint. The squish, squish grew louder and faster, until it no longer seemed connected with his boots. Like a film whose voice track was out of synch with the movements of an actor's lips, the pounding seemed to be coming from elsewhere, from behind, from both left and right, faster and harder than he himself could run. His heart leapt to his throat and stuck there as he forced himself to raise his arms and turn around, half expecting to find an entire pack of cougars converging on him.

He felt his blood drain from his face as a single cougar charged him from where it had cleared the fence after leaving the woods. That spot in the woods where he'd felt its presence for a long time. Its front and back feet worked so swiftly and gracefully he might have appreciated its smooth, cat-like beauty had the look in its eyes not been so coldly and determinedly locked on his eyes. He froze like a statue, his tools dangling helplessly from his half-raised arms. He waited for the impact, the puncture of the teeth through his neck, and death. In his terror, he thought he heard the sounds of another cougar coming from behind.

Just steps from him, the cougar in his sights halted as fast as it had come. Its braking was so sudden that its front paws skidded in the mud. The 100-pound animal spun slightly sideways, sending a spray of dirty water toward him even as it lowered its head and tucked its tail between its legs. For a split second, it looked like a giant kitten who'd cornered a mouse and was moving in for the kill, only to be confronted by a tomcat. Jake's dry mouth fell open as the mountain lion crouched and backed away. He looked at the tools in his hands, wondering if they held a magical power. Then he sensed something behind him and wondered if it was an even larger cougar. As the cat in front of him turned and bounded back toward the woods, he gripped his tools tighter. Every bone in his body trembling, breath all but choked off, he ordered himself to spin around to meet the second, larger attacker. He raised his tools higher and turned. Before him stood the creature whose approach had shaken the ground beneath him in a way that a cougar's soft pads could not have.

He exhaled a long, jagged breath as tears squeezed from the edges of his eyes.

"Hero."

Hero was standing tall, tail erect, ears pointed forward. All 350 pounds of him reeked of an aggression Jake had never seen. From his throat came a rumble Jake had heard only twice before: when Furball had "shot" the eagle, and when Jake had been hit during their nighttime llama-cart ride on the motocross track. But somehow, Jake knew the aggression wasn't for him.

"Hero has adopted you as part of his herd," Sergei had said that day he'd sidehilled down to the sheep field with Eddie and his dad.

Jake dropped his tools to the ground, just to make sure Hero didn't think they were intended for him. Through blurred eyes and a pounding in his ears, he saw and heard the sheep who'd followed their leader across the field. Jake wanted to circle his arms around Hero's neck, sink his face into the matted wool, and let out sobs he was having difficulty holding back. But his instincts told him that just because the big animal had saved his life didn't mean he would tolerate that kind of touching. Guard llamas were chosen for an aggressive streak that they could funnel toward danger once they'd adopted a herd. They weren't as comfortable around humans as other llamas were, nor would a rancher want them to be. It might interfere with their guarding instincts.

"Hero," Jake said again, swallowing and turning his eyes toward the dark forest where the cougar had retreated. "Thank you."

Hero merely turned his long neck toward his flock. The sheep were milling and bleating in confusion in the growing dark and rain, as if requesting reassurance from their tall leader that all was under control.

Jake watched as Hero herded them into a tight pack but hung near the boy. He looked through the fence, saw Sergei's bike parked neatly at the side of the path. But there was no sign of Sergei.

"Sergei!" Jake shouted into the night.

He heard only the pounding of rain into puddles.

He picked up his tools and replaced them in his pack, pulling out his flashlight instead. Moving reluctantly away from Hero, Jake unlatched the gate and stepped through, eyes on the water-filled bike tracks. That's when he saw the tracks of the llama cart. He bent down and shone his flashlight on them. Llamas' split-toed footprints are distinctive, like those of a large deer. He identified some going toward the cabin, and others coming back. So he'd missed Dana for sure. She was on her way to the ranch house.

He squatted down to study the water-filled tracks coming from the cabin. Something was different. What was it? Hey! There were only two sets of llama hoof imprints, as if Salt and Pepper had ditched Furball. But looking closer, he spied Furball's smaller hoof prints on their own, a few feet to one side of the cart's wheel tracks. Like Furball was running alongside or well behind, perhaps on a long lead.

He walked over to Sergei's bike and saw a note stuffed into a plastic sandwich bag and duct-taped to the seat.

"Met Dana," it read. "She's okay but Furball injured. Returning to ranch with her to treat Furball."

Furball was injured? Must've twisted his ankle in a pothole or something. But why would Sergei abandon his motorcycle to ride in the cart? Jake moved closer to the tracks. He scratched his head and looked at Hero as if the llama might offer an explanation. "I'm guessing that Sergei got the insulin to her, but it was so late that she wasn't in good shape. He decided he had to drive and keep an eye on her. He wasn't really going back just to treat Furball." Hero just blinked at Jake. "Anyway, I've missed both of them."

Jake sank wearily onto the wet seat of Sergei's motorcycle. After a few minutes, he threw his leg over it and kicked the starter. The roar was music to his ears. He watched the sheep begin to stampede away from the noise, and Hero, with one more steady look in his direction, follow them.

Now that he had a working bike under him and knew Dana and Sergei were okay, Jake began to relax. Who cared if it was raining? It would be less than an hour's ride to the cabin, with nothing very challenging along the way. It's Dana and Sergei who would have the dicier ride, in the rain on that narrow neck of path behind him. But they'd soon be back in the warmth of the ranch-house kitchen. As for Jake, he'd soon be pulling up to the warmth and good smells of the cabin, where Peter, Levi, and Jerry would be warming up that delicious stew that Dana had just dropped off. His mouth watered as he poured on some speed. Peter had better leave some for him!

19 Mud

Peter wasn't too worried about Jake taking off. He kind of liked being in charge. Too bad these rotten weather conditions limited how fast he and Levi could go and effectively prevented practising any freestyle moves. He couldn't imagine what was holding up Sergei, but it made sense for Jake to do a quick check-up on them in case they needed any help. Peter expected Jake and Sergei to catch up with his trio long before Peter's group neared the cabin. And if they didn't, well—Peter smacked his lips—all the more food for him! Kidding. He'd save them some.

"Sure is getting dark early," he shouted to Jerry as he skidded a little on a corner.

"Yeah. Think we'll get to this cabin before it's totally dark?" The voice revealed apprehension.

Peter wanted to say yes, but he didn't think he should lie. "We'll be okay even if the very last bit is in the dark," he replied with the confidence that a guide should always show his clients.

Jerry nodded soberly and fell in behind Peter on the dusky trail.

"Wish it'd let up a little," Levi complained as he motored forward to ride beside Peter.

"Nah, this is excellent experience for mud-riding in motos," Peter shouted in a cheerful voice with a pasted-on grin.

Levi made a face at him. "In motos, you have pits right beside you in case the mud totally jams up the bike. And this is actually getting beyond what moto-cross race organizers would let people ride in."

"You think so?" Jerry interjected with real worry in his tone now. Peter figured Jerry probably didn't ride often—only to spend time with Levi, and only on easy trails in pleasant weather.

"No way!" Peter said in his upbeat guide's voice. "This is excellent, excellent training. Race you to the showers at the cabin!"

He revved up his motor a little and smiled below his mud-splattered goggles. Levi was as coated in mud as he was. But being a mud monster suited him fine. When he was little, he'd loved rolling down a muddy hill in the rain and returning to his house brown from head to toe. Peter's philosophy was if you're going to get dirty, go for it. Get totally dirty.

He gave his bike a handful of throttle, only to find it was getting tough to tell water from ruts from mud. He tried to recall tips he'd heard for riding in mud. Most of them had to do with parts or maintenance, and he never paid attention to that stuff. Things like spraying electrical parts with something, or changing your tires—that's right, switching to sand tires. Lots of help that was out here. What about advice for actually riding once you're in the stuff? His mind was drawing a blank. Oh well, he thought, I'll just have to rely on my overall superior technique and excellent reaction times.

Whoa! His front wheel caught in a deep rut. He tried to steer out of it, but the clay gave him almost no traction. He slowed a little and tried to ride it out, tried to keep his balance.

What had Sergei told him? That if you're in trouble, the best thing to do is get on the gas. Somehow, that didn't seem right. He sat on the seat and stuck both feet out to the side like outriggers. Maybe if the rut was straight, he could ride it out.

Yikes! He'd hit something, hadn't he? The bike was slowing and the front wheel didn't feel right, even when he gave it more gas. That could only mean a flat tire. No! As he came to a stop, he reached down and gave the front tire a squeeze. His chest felt hollow as the rubber squished in his hands. "No air in the front tire," he wailed.

He shouted ahead to Levi and waved an arm to signal Jerry behind him. He let the bike shudder to a halt and dismounted into a puddle that aspired to be a lake.

The water came nearly to the top of his boots, but that wasn't his main concern. He looked back down the trail in hopes of seeing Jake approaching. How was he going to patch a tire without Jake and Jake's tools?

"What's up?" Jerry asked. He'd managed to avoid the rut, somehow, and was idling on slightly higher ground at the edge of the trail.

"Flat tire," Peter said as he pulled and pushed the bike up to join Jerry. His limbs felt heavy and his throat tight.

"That's rotten," Jerry said, pulling up his goggles and wiping his arm across his damp forehead. "Got a spare tube?"

"No, just a patch," Peter said hesitantly. He had patched a tire before on his BMX bike, but he wasn't entirely sure he could do it on a motorcycle, especially in this weather in the near-dark, with Levi and Jerry watching him. "You good at patching?"

He regretted it the minute he'd said it. He was the guide. He shouldn't let a client know he couldn't even patch a tire very well.

"Not really." Jerry was staring at him, eyebrows pinched together.

"Well, I don't mind patching," Peter said airily, "but it's getting awfully dark to be holding us up."

Truth is, the darkness was just an excuse. He was really wishing Sergei or Jake were here. Even Dana. Dana! He hadn't even thought about her for the past half hour. He'd just been into feeling important as the leader. Pretty selfish, Peter, he told himself. As he studied his tire, he felt a wave of shame. Some leader. Even if it were brilliant daylight, he wouldn't be impressing anyone with his tire-changing skills.

"Your system is going to break down at some point unless you two are joined at the hip," Sergei's words floated back to him. How many times had Jake tried to teach him stuff and Peter had ignored him? "Okay, so it serves me right," Peter thought. "I swear I'll pay full attention next time," he vowed. But what about now?

"Peter, you could always hop on the back of mine," Levi offered, standing beside his bike. "Couldn't be that far to the cabin, right? We can come back in the morning and do it."

Peter, helmet off, ran his muddy sleeve across his wet forehead and stared at the bike, then at Levi. He was glad it was too dark now for his clients to see redness working its way up his neck. Rain ran down his helmet and neck, and seeped into his jersey. Okay, Peter, just admit it, he thought silently. You're really not sure you can do it effectively at all, especially with Levi and his dad looking on. They might be able to help, but that would be very embarrassing. You could catch a ride with Levi, but that doesn't look good either.

He looked back down the trail, willing Jake and Sergei to come cruising down it and bail him out. As his eyes searched, he saw something move. Something small and white bounced and skidded down the hillside, then paused on the trail. Then another and another. A pack of rabbits? He squinted harder as the white blobs came faster. No, rabbits don't slide, and rabbits don't travel in massive packs, and rabbits don't pile up in heaps, some as large as boulders.

"Mudslide!" he suddenly screamed as he realized that the entire hillside packed with chalky-colored rocks was oozing down on the trail like an overflowing cup of hot chocolate with marshmallows. "We've got to get out of here, now!"

But Levi and Jerry continued to stare, frozen, their mouths gaping. They stared as if the mudslide was going to restrict itself to the trail thirty feet behind them. Peter could see that the ridge directly above them was beginning to melt away the same way a surf wave collapses in slow motion.

"Levi!" he screamed as he pulled on his helmet, but Levi seemed stricken.

Peter jumped on Levi's bike and kick-started it. That seemed to wake Levi up. As Peter motioned for Levi to climb on behind him, the boy did so in a daze.

"Now, Jerry, go!" Peter screamed.

By now, Jerry had sighted rocks tumbling toward them from directly above. Peter, at the controls of Levi's bike with Levi clutching him from behind, saw Jerry gun it just seconds before one small boulder rolled to where his back tire had just been. Visibly shaking, the man fell into line behind his guide. Peter turned his head back to the front and maneuvered the bike along to the right edge of the trail. The slide was depositing mud, rocks, and debris on the path, faster and faster—but so far, none was spilling up on the far edge.

It forced Peter to follow a very fine line: the high, less muddy edge of the trail near where it plunged down a hillside to the right. If Peter could just hug that edge until they were away from the steep bank on their left, they'd be okay. And if Jerry could manage to follow, they might clear out of this danger zone before a more ambitious mudslide decided to scoop them up and spill them into the woods below, maybe slamming rocks into their heads along the way.

Peter switched on his headlights, mentally thanking Sergei for having taken the precaution of outfitting the bikes with them. He hated how heavy Levi's bike felt with two on board. It made not getting stuck in the mud a major challenge. Every few moments, he wobbled like a high-wire acrobat, but he gritted his teeth and carried on. Talk to it, he told himself. Do the body and soul thing. In moments, it would be so dark that it would be a miracle if they didn't crash into one of the obstacles being flung down the hill toward them. But he was a motocross racer, a freestyle guy, and a dirt-bike guide. He could do it. He had to do it.

Within moments, it was pitch-black, but the mudslide seemed to be behind them. Peter slowed, stared, and listened. They were resting on a high point; there was no longer any terrain to his left to slide into the road. The mud wave had spent itself, and his guess was that they were now very close to the cabin.

"Thanks for getting us out of there, Peter," Jerry said, visibly shaking. "I hope it's not far now."

"Good biking, Jerry," Peter replied, turning and smiling. "We've done the worst stuff, and the cabin is just around a few corners. Take 'em slow."

He waited until Jerry nodded before moving down the next hill. The weak pool of light from his headlight was annoying and almost useless. But it was indeed better than nothing. Once, it identified a small log lying diagonally across the trail, allowing him to steer around it.

"Good eye," Levi shouted encouragingly into his ear as Peter turned to make sure Jerry, too, managed to skirt it.

Peter let out a joyous shout when his headlight picked up the outline of the cabin. He leapt off and shook Levi's, then Jerry's hands. They cut their motors and Peter pulled a flashlight from his zippered pouch. "Way to go, Mr. Morgan. You totally stayed with us."

"Nice guiding," Jerry returned, his face relaxing.

"Thanks for taking over," Levi said, head hanging a little as if embarrassed he'd needed Peter to do so.

"No problem," Peter replied, but his head was cocked toward where the lower trail approached the cabin. "Shhh. Listen!" he said.

20   The Cabin

As he motored up a final rise, Jake was disappointed to see no lights shining from the cabin. Then he spotted a flashlight's beam moving around on the porch. He pulled up, cut his motor, and was greeted by Peter's voice.

"Jake, old buddy! You made it! So you ended up coming on the lower trail! Just as well. Should've seen the mudslide we outrode on the upper! Hey, what took you so long? We got held up 'cause of a flat tire. Can you believe this rain? So did you see Dana? How is she? And where's Sergei? Is everything okay?"

Jake smiled as he got off his bike and took long strides toward the protection of the porch. "Peter, it's rude to ask ninety-nine questions at once, especially when our clients are shivering in this rain. Let's get inside and get that fire and stew going. Sergei and Dana are fine, and I get first dibs on the shower after Mr. Morgan and Levi."

Jerry laughed. "And Levi definitely goes first because I can't even tell he's my son with all that mud on him. You're all muddier than me, that's for sure!"

Jake was pleased to see Jerry looking relaxed, and Peter and Levi in one piece. He counted only two motorcycles. He figured they'd left the third one parked around the side of the cabin.

Everyone tugged their boots and the worst of their muddy gear off and draped it over the porch's railing as Peter unlocked the front door and hit the A-frame's light switches. The cabin transformed instantly into a warm, cozy place. Now, the steady downpour faded to a sort of musical rhythm on the steep roof. Jake struck a match and touched it to the shredded newspaper that Dana had expertly arranged under the kindling and logs in the fireplace. Levi beelined for the shower.

"Wow, so nice to have our clothes and sleeping bags right here on the beds waiting for us," Jerry called from one of the bedrooms. "Even fluffy towels." He emerged a minute later in dry clothing with a smile on this face. "Back-of-Beyond Ranch rocks."

Jake smiled as he ignited the stove element under the big pot of stew. He lifted the lid and sniffed.

"Mmmm." Then he spotted the tray of cheese and crackers Dana had set out, removed its plastic wrap, and offered it to Jerry like he was a butler in a classy hotel, never mind that he stood shirtless and barefoot in muddy trousers.

"Why, thank you, sir," Jerry said, eagerly fitting a wedge of cheese onto a cracker and lifting it to his lips. "So you were going to tell us about Sergei and Dana?"

"Yeah, tell us," Peter said, lowering the tray.

Jake told his story and heard Peter's in return, with quick breaks for each member of the party to slip into and out of the shower. Jake couldn't believe how good it felt to emerge from his and Peter's room with clean, warm clothes and freshly washed hair. With effort, he'd scrubbed the cold, the wet, the mud, and the fright of the cougar encounter from his mind.

"I'm ravenous," he announced.

"I'm Peter," Peter responded, ladling up the stew into bowls on the table.

"It's still pouring," Levi observed as they lit into the flavorful meat stew, chock-full of potatoes and vegetables from Natalia's garden.

"That mudslide was amazing," Jerry mused between spoonfuls.

"The hillside, it is fallen!" Peter squeaked in a high voice with a sly smile at Jake.

Jake grinned as he pictured the hillside sliding down over the path like chocolate soufflé over a baking pan. "He's mimicking Natalia," he explained to Levi and his dad. "That's what she always says about stuff that comes out of her oven."

Jerry reached for the loaf of bread on the table and busied himself carving a slice from it. "Well, if this came out of her oven, I would vigorously disagree with her view of her own cooking."

Jake didn't respond because the mental snapshot of the mudslide Peter had encountered made his mind jump to that narrow neck that Sergei and Dana would have had to cross in the rain. Llamas, he told himself, could go where horses couldn't. Their long, split toes gave them a confident grip on almost any terrain. Jake's spoon froze halfway to his mouth. *Almost* any terrain *but mud*, Sergei had told them.

Jake turned to stare out the dark window at the sheets of rain. Sergei would have intercepted Dana shortly after it started raining, but the two must have left the lower trail's treehouse heading for the ranch about the time of Peter's mudslide. What if they'd gotten caught by something like that?

"Jake, what are you thinking about?" Jerry asked. "Here we are in a first-class cabin with a gourmet dinner and a fireplace just waiting for popcorn, and you look like you've lost your best friend."

"Sorry," he said, but he pushed his chair back and walked to the window, unable to wipe a frown from his face. He cupped his hands around his eyes, pressed his face to the cold glass of the window, and peered out into the dark. Nothing but dark, wet, and the eerie black outline of trees waving in the wind. Then a white face rose from nowhere and pressed itself against the other side of the glass. The black eyes that stared into Jake's were huge and inhuman. He screamed as he jumped back.

"What the devil …?" Peter asked, his chair screeching as he leapt up and joined Jake. "Oh no! Where'd he come from?!"

By now, Levi and Jerry had also rushed to the window.

"I don't see anything!" Levi cried.

But Jake had sprinted to the cabin's cupboard and grabbed an old ice cream bucket with a fitted lid. He ran to the front door and flung it open. Then he walked slowly and cautiously toward Furball, one hand lifting the lid on the llama-food container.

"What's that? What're you doing?" Levi asked.

"Bucket of llama grain. Sergei and Dana always fetch it to feed them when we're here," he replied. His eyes fastened on the llama's trailing rope.

"Stay back," he advised the trio who were crowding the doorway behind him. "I'll get him. Furball," he called in a soft voice as he held up the tin. "Furball, old buddy. Hungry?"

Furball, standing warily on three legs, the fourth lifted up and trembling a little, looked forlorn in his mud-spattered coat. But one ear pricked forward, the other back as he surveyed Jake's bucket.

"Come on, boy. You poor thing. You've hurt your leg, and you're out here all alone. I know you don't like rain," Jake coaxed while looking hopefully around the dark, empty yard for a llama cart, a person, Salt, or Pepper.

"What's he doing …?" Peter's voice came from the doorway.

"Shhh," Jake scolded Pete. "He seems kind of agitated. He's upset or something."

Furball was milling back and forth, his head tossing from side to side. He pawed the boards of the front porch. But his eyes kept returning to the bucket. Jake lifted a fistful of grain from it, set the container down on the porch, and extended his hand patiently toward the llama. At last, Furball limped across the porch and sank his muzzle into it. Jake enjoyed the warm feeling of the llama's nose snuffling hungrily about his hand, but he knew better than to stroke Furball's neck. Anyway, there wasn't time. Moving slowly, he lowered his free hand to clutch Furball's dangling rope.

"It's frayed, not cut," he said to Peter, who moved forward to examine it.

"He chewed through it," Peter ruled as Jake nodded soberly.

"What does that mean?" Levi asked.

"It means he was in some kind of danger," Jake said huskily. "It means Dana and Sergei might be in trouble," he added, hearing his voice wobble as his fist clenched the llama's rope.

Everyone peered into the wet darkness. But there was only the splat of rain on mud.

"It'd be risky to go back out." Jerry Morgan commented, in a slightly higher voice than usual.

"If Furball escaped some disaster, then Sergei and Dana might have," Peter's voice asserted.

"We don't know how long it's taken Furball to get here, especially with a bad leg," Jake reasoned.

"And that's assuming he came straight here and didn't wander around first," Levi commented.

Jake coaxed Furball toward a porch post, where he tied the end of the rope securely. Swiftly now, Jake turned to his three companions backlit by the cabin doorway's glow.

"Mr. Morgan and Levi, you'll be okay here without us. Peter and I have to go after Sergei and Dana in case they need help." He grabbed some gas containers from under the porch and began filling up his and Peter's tanks.

Jerry nodded his head, his eyes big. He opened his

mouth as if to ask something, but closed it again and placed an arm around Levi's shoulders.

"Let me help fill your tanks," Levi offered. "And take my bike, Peter."

Jake was half surprised Levi didn't offer to accompany them on his dad's bike, but Jake would have had to give a firm no, since Sergei would never approve of his junior guides needlessly endangering clients on what might be a dodgy rescue mission. Besides, Levi probably knew his nervous father needed someone with him in the cabin.

"Thanks," Peter said, pulling on his gear and helmet in synch with Jake. "Sorry, Levi, but I think you understand."

"Go!" Levi urged him, nodding. "Furball and we will be fine."

"Give Furball food and water but don't try to pet him," Peter instructed him.

Jake brought his bike to life with a roar, and performed a tight U-turn to point it back down the lower trail. "Got your fanny pack?" he shouted at Peter, even as he noted it slung around his friend's waist.

"Yup!"

The rain was definitely slackening, much to Jake's relief. Whatever damage had been done to the lower trail was probably all that would occur that night.

"Watch out for rocks and keep your speed down," Jake shouted. Peter nodded and fell in behind him. Even though the trail was wide, straight, and flat on this section, the mud made it treacherous at any speed. Jake forced himself to stay in a higher gear than he normally would use to keep the rear tire from spinning. Slow and steady is better than slipping and crashing, he told himself.

Their headlights seemed inadequate for helping them negotiate the muddy, rock-infested trail safely. He could hardly believe Peter had managed to do the last portion of the upper trail in the dark—in much heavier rain, and carrying the extra weight of Levi. Jake felt his stomach tighten even thinking about that challenge. Better Peter than him for that feat; Peter's bike handling abilities had gotten them to safety. Then again, Jake thought with a grimace, if Peter had been able to patch his tire before it had fallen dark—as Jake would have—that wouldn't have happened. There'd been time. Only barely before that mudslide hit, Peter had confided to him, but enough time for a fast fix. Of course, Jake had refrained from rubbing it in. The way Peter's head had hung when he'd said that, Jake knew his friend had learned a lesson. Anyway, who was Jake to talk? He'd had to ditch his own bike because of his failure at remembering sidehilling technique. He'd been too busy following others down the hill the previous time, instead of memorizing what he might need to know if on his own.

"Mechanics isn't everything," Dana had said.

"Think of Alley Seymour," Peter had tweaked him. "An ex-pro racer who became a famous mechanic for Kevin Windham. He knew his stuff *on* the bike before he went for full-time in the pits. That's the kind of wrencher racers will fight over."

Jake flinched and braked as he felt his tire fishtail on a bend, sending a rock spitting back toward Peter. Slow and steady. Slow and steady, he told himself. But as he glanced at the inky outline of trees around them and thought of the cougar, he sped up just a little again.

21   To the Rescue

By the time they pulled up to take a breather in front of the treehouse, the rain had stopped altogether. Peter cast his beam around.

"No sign of Hero or his sheep across the way," he reported.

They revved their motors and surged onward, playing dodge ball with rocks strewn about the path. Jake had let Peter ahead to lead, as if expecting an increasingly technical ride. Until now, the terrain to their right had been a gentle rise, sloping right up through forest or field to the upper trail. Here, however, the hill became sharply steeper. Were they safe from any new mudslides as they rode on down the trail? The rain had stopped, so Peter hoped the danger was small, but his jaw tightened just contemplating the risk.

When he came to the first small tree across the

path, Peter accelerated, pulling on the handlebars slightly. The front wheel cleared the log, which acted like a jump for the rear wheel. He landed beautifully, then looked behind to make sure Jake had managed to do the same.

"Way to go," he shouted with a thumbs-up. He'd always known Jake had it in him. His buddy was rising to the occasion.

When he had to veer suddenly to avoid some newly exposed tree roots, Peter flashed a hand signal to Jake, then turned briefly to make sure Jake hadn't gotten caught. Soon they began encountering the remains of mini-slides. They resembled whoops embedded with rocks and sticks. Peter slowed just enough to ensure that none of the protruding sticks would catch in his spokes. "Like whoops full of half-buried, giant porcupines," he mumbled.

He kept glancing backwards and feeling an ever-growing sense of pride in Jake's biking. They passed the treehouse without pause. Soon they were nearing the narrowest neck. As they came around the bend, Peter stopped dead and gaped. He and Jake stared at what their headlights illuminated only dimly. It was as if a wall of wet dirt had been dumped by a giant dump truck for a future construction job. Sitting before them was a blockade the width of two semi-trucks, and maybe two and a half stories high, rising up at the same angle as a ramp in a freestyle event. Worse, it had more sticks, stones, and stumps than Natalia's best cookies had chocolate chips. After suffocating the trail, it had oozed right over the edge of the cliff—hopefully long after the cart had passed by, Peter thought as his stomach tightened. Where on earth had this monstrosity come from? Okay, stupid question. It was the remains of the bluff on the right, which now had a giant cleft in it.

Peter hadn't really processed the danger he'd been in on the upper trail when he—with Levi clinging to him—had accelerated out of the way of that slow-moving slide. A mudslide on this section could only be far swifter and deadlier than the one they'd outrun. Peter had watched enough television footage of what reporters called "debris slides" to know that some move slowly enough to outrun, and others can bury an entire town in seconds. He'd even seen news clips of slides smashing houses into splinters and cartwheeling uprooted trees like toothpicks. He remembered one particularly harrowing TV clip where they'd pulled a woman out of a house that had been taken right off its foundations. She'd ended up with debris pinning her entire body, but her head had come to rest in an air pocket, and a dog had led rescuers to her in time.

He wished they had Scout with them.

"Sergei! Dana!" Peter yelled as he sprang from his motorcycle and began trying to climb the mountain. Of course, the mud slid him right back to the ground.

"Dana! Sergei!" Jake shouted even louder, running back and forth the length of the barrier with a flashlight from his pack trained on the mud.

Peter tackled the hill once again, this time pulling himself up one handhold at a time on the branches sticking from the mud. "No sign of them," he panted from the top of the hump. He soon finished pacing its entire length, aiming his beam on every possible pocket, both sides. If they were buried, he was certain that something would show: a hand, a piece of cart, a llama hoof, right?

"What do we do?" Jake shouted up to him from where their motorcycles remained parked.

Peter, still on top of the mound, turned to look down at the far side, trying to make his flashlight pierce the darkness of the trail on the other side, but he could see nothing. Slowly, he lowered his beam, then slid down to Jake.

"This thing tapers at the top," he informed Jake, "like a tabletop jump. If we roar up there, we can catch our breath before we slither down the far side. I think we can be pretty sure they're not trapped under here. We need to push on, fast."

"We'll never be able to drag our bikes up there. Or get anywhere quickly if we ditch them here and walk," Jake agreed.

Peter nodded soberly and mounted his motorcycle. The hand on his throttle itched. He turned to Jake. He could see Jake's widened eyes right through Jake's goggles. He waited for his friend to finish examining the blockade.

"So you're going to do it?" Jake asked in a low, steady voice.

"Yes," Peter replied resolutely.

"I'll wait till you're safely at the top," Jake said, jaw lifted and set.

Peter nodded soberly. It was important that Jake didn't follow too closely, in case Peter slipped and slid down on him.

"Uphills are mostly about power and balance, Jake. Look for the straightest route, build momentum, and hit it in a gear that gives you lots of revs. I'd say third gear, except on this slide, we've gotta watch for the obstacles in the mud. Stay loose when you start up it, then constantly shift body position, whatever you need for traction. Keep the front wheel on the ground!"

As Jake nodded, Peter knew he was taking it in this time, taking it in as if his life, or maybe someone else's, depended on it.

"And if I need to bail?" Jake asked.

"Jump off the bike to the side."

"And when I get to the top?" he asked.

Peter was impressed. Jake was clearly listening and asking smart questions. "Lower the front end fast."

"Like, let off the gas and lean forward?"

"You've got it. But not so much that you endo. And keep moving once you land so you can get away from the loose ground where you might otherwise slide backward. Then slow it down and stay off your front brake when you go down the other side."

He waited until Jake nodded. "You can do it, Jake."

"I know," Jake said. Peter liked Jake's determined tone.

Peter turned around to get a head start. Then he circled and flew at it as if he were approaching the ramp at a freestyle event. He knew this would be much more slippery than anything he'd faced, and that doing it in the pitch-black was an act of extreme desperation. He knew it was full of sharp objects that could knock him off his intended course, rip his flesh, or break a bone if he fell. But he'd scouted with his light and picked out a route. The only big scare was knowing that the mudslide might still be unstable. Ripping up the slope of the cliff's freshly spilled guts might actually make it gush more. But he had to take that chance. Sergei and Dana might be in danger further ahead. He dared not waste another second.

He sped toward the hump, heart racing faster than the bike. He held his breath as his trusty 125 hit and slithered up the ramp he'd chosen, at break-neck speed. He followed his carefully selected path, second by second. He maintained a steady throttle, moving his body forward and back to keep his rear wheel hooked up, and his front from wheeling. Teeth clenched, knees slightly bent out, he let his mind send urgent messages to the machine beneath him: "Yes, yes, yes you can! Up, up, up you go! I'm with you, I'm with you, watch that stump, we're nearly there, hang on!"

Sergei had said he should talk to his machine and embrace its body and soul. Okay, he'd do it! Whatever worked! Like a rocket clearing its launch pad, he flew all but vertically up that slope, caught a bit of air at the top, then landed softly on the glimmer of table-top: the muddiest, messiest, briefest tabletop he'd ever had the misfortune of meeting. The bike tried to slide out from under him, but every muscle and sinew in Peter's body was on full duty. He kept it together, desperately trying to slow before topping the crown. But even with his right hand riding the brake and his boots deliberately dragging in the mud to help, he found himself slithering over the far edge. His teeth ground as he saw he was committed downward now.

His meager headlight shone down the far side of the bank, illuminating the route he'd picked out earlier.

His attempt at braking prompted him to slither dangerously sideways. He had a choice of falling and rolling, or lurching ahead and trying to convert his descent into a sidehilling maneuver. Hoping Jake wouldn't come careening down on top of him, he tried for the sidehilling. He was concentrating on staying centered and watching for logs and boulders, all the while trying to swallow his panic, when the bike finally completed its runout. He braked hard on the goopy trail and turned his head to the sound of Jake's engine.

Jake was standing on top of the barrier beside his bike, using its headlight to scout. He stood there a long time before starting down. Peter stared up to see Jake sidehilling like a pro, on a zigzaggy, compressed-mud terrace that seemed to have been laid out for him. Whoa, was that really Jake? Where had he learned that kind of gutsiness and control? And way to pick a line.

When he saw that Jake was going to make it, Peter raised his arm in the air and shouted "yes!" Their gloved hands met in a victory slap. Then they forged ahead on the dark lower trail. Only to meet a second, equally massive mud barrier within a hundred feet.

"No!" Peter shouted, cutting his engine once again.

But this time he lost no time dismounting and groping his way up it, eyes all around looking for any sign of cart or body parts poking through the mud. Once on top, he walked the full length of its spine, stepping gingerly. "Please don't be buried beneath me," he whispered. "Be back at the ranch safe."

Before he'd walked the hump's full slippery length, however, his beam picked up a pool of white on the far side, directly beneath him. The white made for an alarming contrast with the pitch-black of the mud and the night, and it could be only one thing: the kneeling body of Salt, the llama.

"Jake! I found Salt!" he screamed as he cast his beam about and slid down to the animal.

Seconds later, Peter was kneeling beside Salt, who sat like a sphinx in front of a pyramid, with his knees tucked under him, his rump just inches forward of the slide. The animal raised his head and made a donkey-like braying noise as he tried to rise. Peter saw that, although the slide had missed him, it had buried the cart and his harness, holding him prisoner in his kneeling position. As Peter whipped out his knife and cut Salt free, he saw twisted portions of the cart sticking up from the mud like arms trying to reach forward around the giant trunk of a fallen tree. The half-buried tree, he realized, must have slid into the cart like a semi-truck into a bike at an intersection. At least the slide hadn't taken the cart and llamas over the nearby drop-off.

The braying of another llama turned his head. At first he thought Pepper, being black, was half-buried by the mud. But once he'd brushed his arm across Pepper's hindquarters, he found that, again, it was only Pepper's mud-anchored lines holding him down. By the time he'd cut these free and Pepper had struggled to his feet, Jake had scrambled down to help.

"Sergei! Dana!" they shouted as they trained their lights up the slope and along the massive tree trunk. With bare hands, they began digging like dogs. They dug in the slide wherever a portion of the llama cart poked up. It was like digging at the beach to unearth a stick that turned out to be part of an entire root system.

"The cart is totally bent and contorted," Jake cried, desperation in his voice. "Unless they were thrown clear …"

"Jake?" a weak female voice called out from somewhere nearby.

Peter and Jake leapt up and rushed to where the voice had come from on the other side of the half-buried tree.

Together, they leapt over the tree and pooled their lights on Dana's face. A shock traveled down Peter's spine as he realized nothing was visible but her face. Many a time at the beach, Peter had enjoyed being buried up to his neck by his dad on summer days. They'd use shovels and hands to excavate as big a hole as they could. Then, giggling, Peter would lower himself in and beg his dad to push the final pile of sand to his neck to trap him. After a couple of minutes, of course, one yelp from Peter would have his dad scooping the sand away to free his grinning son.

But seeing Dana firmly trapped, her face and wet, dark hair so smudged with dirt that it was difficult to see her in the night, sent a bolt of horror and panic through Peter. Like Jake, he dived over to her and began pulling, pulling the mud away. It was tightly packed, but not impossible to claw away in wet clumps.

"Sergei," she said in a voice that sounded like her very voicebox was compressed by the mud avalanche.

"Sergei," Peter repeated, lowering his face closer to hers. "Where is he?"

"I don't know. I've called and called for him." She tried to twist her neck as the boys cleared more and more mud away from her. "Find Sergei," she begged in that same weak voice.

"Not till we've freed your arms and your pack," Jake spoke up sternly, mud flying away from his fingers.

She didn't argue, especially since they were seconds away from freeing her torso. As soon as her left arm was free, she even started helping them, clawing almost absent-mindedly as her glazed eyes looked about. But as they began pulling dirt away from her right arm, she screamed.

"I think it's broken or something," she said, wincing.

Peter dug more gently, trying not to touch it.

"Water?" Dana asked after a second, her tongue running around the mud that caked her mouth.

Peter jumped up and dashed to his motorcycle to retrieve his bottle. He held it to her lips and watched her drink greedily from it. Droplets coursing down her chin took some of the mud with them.

By the time she was finished, Jake had both her arms unpinned. She held the right tight against her chest while making a brave effort to help the boys reach her fanny pack with her left.

"How long have you been here?" Peter asked Dana.

"I don't know," she replied, shivering. "Hours."

The second Jake and Peter had freed her to her waist and unbuckled her fanny pack, she pushed the fumbling fingers of her left hand toward it. Peter watched Jake unzip it for her and close his fingers around what he guessed she needed: the little box of orange juice. Her eyes thanked Jake and Peter as she stuffed the juice box's straw into it and began to sip greedily. When she'd finished, she began laying out what she needed for her blood test, one-handed.

Though she was still shaking a little, Peter judged her able to do that on her own. So, keeping one eye on her, he raised his stiff body and looked about.

"Sergei!"

22   The Dig

Peter started to walk the debris slowly, in concentric circles, training his light on anything that might reveal Sergei's whereabouts. He almost missed the sight of a sleeve sticking up out of the mud like a lost handkerchief in between rocks and sticks. It was only two feet from the thick trunk of the felled tree at whose other end they'd discovered Dana. And it was uncomfortably close to where the slide plunged over the cliff. Peter's heart twisted as both dread and hope filled him.

"Jake, help me!" Peter shouted, diving to his knees and throwing up panicked fistfuls of mud. He clawed on either side of the sleeve, pulling soil away even faster than he had around Dana. Sure enough, it was a motocross jersey, encased around a mud-trapped human arm. Even as he cupped Sergei's hand in his, Peter determined it still had some warmth in it.

"Jake!" Peter screamed again. "It's Sergei!" Jake appeared and dropped down beside him as both threw their entire bodies into removing dirt. They excavated the arm from wrist to elbow to shoulder, only to be stopped by the tree trunk.

Now they dug like badgers determined to make a home under that tree. They removed the dirt from around Sergei's shoulders and reached the back of his neck.

"Dig faster!" Jake shouted.

Suddenly, the mud around Sergei's head seemed to come free easily—too easily. Peter grabbed an extra-large handful, then lost his balance and fell forward. Way forward. "Help!" Peter shouted as he felt himself tumble into a hollow under the log. The section of mud on which he'd been kneeling had collapsed into a sort of giant bubble in the slide: like an underground cave beneath the tree.

An air pocket! As Peter rolled onto his back, he let out a sharp cry at the astonishing sight of Sergei's white face and closed eyes suspended immediately over him in the cavity.

Jake, his hands cupped around Sergei's chin to support his head, called down, "Are you okay, Peter?"

"Uh-huh." Peter rose to position an ear under the man's mouth. "He's breathing," Peter declared, his own heart pounding faster.

"Sergei, Sergei, are you okay?" he and Jake chorused together. There was no reply. Peter hadn't really expected one. Digging his fingernails into the palms of his hands and looking at Jake, he tried to recall the first aid training they'd been required to take as junior guides for Sam's Adventure Tours.

"Okay," Peter began, "we have an unconscious victim who is breathing."

"That means no mouth-to-mouth resuscitation …" Jake recited.

"And no whomping on his chest to get his heart started again," Peter finished.

"That's cardiopulmonary resuscitation—CPR," Jake reminded him.

"Whatever. We need to make sure he's warm enough, and we need to make sure we don't move his neck or spine in case they're injured."

"Yes," Jake said. He was stretched on his stomach in the mud beside Sergei, still cupping his hands around Sergei's face.

"We need to uncover the rest of him to make sure he's not bleeding," Peter suggested.

"And get to the ranch to call emergency services …"

"We could drape him over a llama …"

"That wouldn't be keeping his neck and spine straight."

"That's true."

They both looked up as Dana walked unsteadily over the mud toward them, right arm still held fast against her chest. She'd stuffed Peter's water bottle between her fanny pack and waist. She bent down. Peter was impressed she'd finished digging herself out with one arm. He was also relieved she wasn't too injured to walk. But she was swaying a little dizzily. "Sergei," she said, just as her boots slipped out from under her and landed her in the pocket under the log, beside Peter.

She screamed, curled up, and clutched one arm with the other, tears squeezing out of her eyes.

"Dana, are you okay?" Peter reached out to help her sit up, carefully avoiding her bad arm.

"I'm fine," she said between clenched teeth after several heaves of breath, "just tired. I slipped. No big deal. He's breathing?"

"Yes."

"But unconscious?"

The boys nodded.

She rose to a kneeling position and spied Salt and Pepper, who'd come to investigate the pile of human beings halfway up the mud hump. They shook their long necks and fastened their eyes on Sergei's still form. Dana shifted to a crouch and looked over the rim of the hole to gaze at the llamas.

"They're okay," Peter reassured her. "And so is Furball."

Dana struggled to stand but slipped again, this time hitting Sergei's shoulder on the way down. A groan came from his lips.

They all turned. Peter was astonished to see Sergei's eyes open.

"Sergei!" he cried, hands reaching for one of the man's arms.

Sergei muttered something Peter couldn't make out. Peter leaned in closer. "Sergei?"

"Water," came the word again.

Of course! Peter grabbed the water bottle from Dana and moved it toward Sergei's lips, but how was he going to get water into him when the rancher was on his stomach and they weren't supposed to move his neck?

Luckily, the bottle had a squirt top on it, and Sergei seemed satisfied to have it spouted up into his mouth, so Peter kept squirting at intervals as the man grunted his thanks. Meantime, Dana had crawled out of the hole and was digging to uncover Sergei's lower body. When Sergei was finished drinking, Peter joined in as Jake continued to support the man's neck. The minute Peter and Dana had uncovered him, all three teens jumped back as Sergei unexpectedly rolled himself over and sat up.

"Sergei!" Peter objected. "You shouldn't do that! Your spine might …"

"I am perfectly okay!" Sergei roared, grabbing Peter's water bottle and draining it like a cowboy who'd sauntered into a bar for whiskey. "And you're okay," he said, eyes settling on Dana. "Except for your arm. Broken?"

Before she could respond, a soft braying noise sounded. Sergei's head swiveled toward Salt and Pepper. "And darned if our llama team isn't on the loose and looking undamaged, except for needing a good wash. Wait. Where's Furball?" His eyes swept the dark around him. "Where in tarnation is our limping devil? He'd better not have been buried! I've invested way too much in his rehab!"

"Furball is at the cabin. Jerry and Levi are looking after him," Peter informed Sergei.

"He made it to the cabin?" Dana asked incredulously.

"The little devil chewed partway through his leash while I was clearing a rock from the path, minutes before the mudslide hit," Sergei told them.

"We figured it wasn't enough that he could break away, so we kept going," Dana explained.

"But he broke clean away and bolted backwards just as Salt and Pepper bolted forwards. Almost like all three knew what was coming," Sergei said.

"And we got caught in the middle and buried," Dana said, her voice catching.

"But not pulled over the cliff," Jake spoke up. "And Furball must've gotten past where the second landslide hit before it came down."

"What second landslide?" Sergei asked.

The boys told them about the landslide they'd biked over just yards before this one. The rancher and farmhand said nothing. They just stared at where their own mudslide plunged over the cliff's edge barely a stone's throw away.

"When Furball showed up, we knew you were in trouble," Peter continued. "That's why we rode down here fast as we could. Think Furball knew to come find us to help you?"

At this, Sergei guffawed loudly. "Furball? That little monster just wanted to get out of the rain. The cabin porch was the perfect rain shelter."

"Too bad he didn't at least try to climb up our mudslide first, to help dig you two out," Jake commented.

"He's a berserk llama, not Lassie the dog," Dana replied dryly, lifting her good arm to rub a patch of mud off her cheeks as if she'd only just realized how filthy she was.

"I'm surprised Salt and Pepper didn't chew through their harnesses," Peter said, as it suddenly occurred to him to pull granola bars from his pack and pass them all around.

"They had way too many to get through, but they might have done it eventually," Sergei said, scarfing his granola bar while sliding on his muddy buttocks down to where their harnesses and a portion of the cart stuck out of the slide. "Dana, stay put. I'll deal with your arm in a minute. But Peter, get over here. I need your light. I'm amazed they didn't take off after you cut their harnesses. Must've thought we were highly entertaining." The tone of his voice changed as he called to them. "Good boys, easy now," he said, catching their trailing nose halters one by one. He limped to a nearby tree, buckled his fanny pack around it, and tied up the llama's short leads. He uttered what Peter figured must be a Russian curse. "It's going to cost me to replace these. But maybe I can mend them."

"Sorry about cutting them, Sergei," Peter said, laughing as he realized the Russian was fully himself if he was worrying about the cost of llama harnesses right after nearly losing his life.

Then Peter turned serious. "Sergei, you really shouldn't be standing up and moving around. You don't know you haven't hurt your back or something."

Sergei turned and looked at Peter. "Do I look like

anything is wrong with me?" he boomed. "*Gloopy* boys. I'm a vet, a type of doctor. Let's start hauling this cart out of the mud, okay? Then you have to get back to the cabin."

He stopped and stared up at the mudslide as if seeing it for the first time. "You boys biked over one like this?"

"Yup, just a hundred yards behind this one," Peter said proudly. "Our bikes are parked the other side of this one."

Sergei stared at them. "Think you'll be okay for making it back up and over that other slide, then? You need to get back to the clients quickly."

"Of course," Jake said, drawing himself up tall.

"Well then," Sergei said, pulling his eyes back to the ends of the harnesses. He ran his hands up to where the leather disappeared into the mud. He started to tug and dig, then paused to look up at his workers.

"What a mess this is going to be for the Forest Service to clear. We should probably offer my Bobcat to help them."

Dana's laugh from the mud hole made Peter and Jake look up.

"Sergei, you're worrying about cleanup already?"

He smiled and clambered toward her. Peter heard him quizzing her about her arm and heard her cry out "ouch!" once.

"Broken, for sure. And your throttle arm, of all things. Well"—Peter heard the sound of duct tape being pulled off a roll—"we'll make sure it doesn't move on the way back to the ranch. Then I'll make you a cast. They're just cotton and bandages soaked in plaster of Paris, you know. I've made 'em lots of times for animals with broken legs."

"You're not going to have a doctor do it?" Peter dared to ask as he and Jake continued digging out the cart.

"I'll let a doctor X-ray it, but I can do the cast," Sergei boasted. "Casts on a throttle arm have to be specially sculpted around the wrist to let the person still work the throttle, you know. Good thing she didn't break her right leg. That would mean rigging up an electric starter!"

Peter and Jake looked at each other and grinned. They heard Dana giggling.

"Boys! Dig faster!" Sergei called out as he kept winding duct tape from Dana's arm, up around her shoulder, down her back, and back again. "I'll help you dig in a second. Then I'm counting on Jake and his fancy fix-it skills to put the cart back to working order. Enough to get Dana and me out of here, anyway. After that, you boys head back to the cabin, *da*? Slowly, carefully. They are our paying customers, you know."

With his big arms around Dana's good side, he helped steer her down the pile of mud, where both of them joined the boys in excavating the cart. "I'm gonna escort this llama driver and her pair of animals back home, where I've half a mind to let Natalia fix me up something good to eat and put me to bed. I'll be up at the crack of dawn, though, to join you at the cabin," he said, glancing back up the mudslide.

"You don't need to come in the morning," Jake said.

"Oh yes we do," Dana spoke up. "To collect Furball."

"That little escape-artist devil," Sergei added.

No more so than Sergei and Dana themselves, Peter reflected as he neared the end of a llama-cart archaeological dig with his and Jake's newly unearthed comrades.

23 Clients

"So then you bent the llama cart back into shape enough they could ride in it, and they took off for the ranch again?" Jerry was saying, shaking his head as he looked out the cabin's window into the blackness of the night. "Bet Natalia was relieved to see them."

"Bet she was," Peter agreed.

"What a story," Jerry said, sitting down on the cabin's sofa in his plaid flannel pajamas and giant slippers. To Jake, he looked relaxed and happy for the first time all week.

Jake fetched butter from the cabin's little refrigerator, but he wasn't sure he was going to be able to eat any popcorn. Not after downing a bowl of leftover stew, two of the cinnamon buns intended for breakfast, half a dozen roasted marshmallows, and a cup of cocoa. But hey, the clients had voted for popcorn, and it was his duty as a junior guide to join them. He stuck his own slippered feet up on the hearth and dove his hand into the bowl.

"Levi," Peter was carrying on, "if you ever need a lesson on sidehilling in extremely muddy conditions, ask Jake. He was awesome up there. A total professional coming down that mudslide."

"Yeah, well my bike is still in the sheep field waiting for pick up after my previous sidehilling attempt," Jake tossed back. "I guess practise makes perfect. It was getting *up* that mound that was sketchy, not coming down." The truth was, he was kind of proud of himself. For once, he'd listened to Peter's advice and used it.

"Sketchy? I thought it was fun. Hope my next freestyle event is rainy so I can demonstrate that again," Peter boasted as he leaned his head back and dropped fluffy, freshly buttered popcorn into his mouth, one kernel at a time.

"But it never rains here in summer," Levi panned. "Hardly ever, anyway."

"And cougars never stalk people who weigh more than 100 pounds," Jake inserted, making a face at Levi.

"And berserk llamas can't chew through their leashes, predict mudslides, or find their way to our cabin," Peter piped up, one eye on the front window.

"Then there are berserk dirt bikers," Jerry joined in. "Can they really outrun small mudslides and jump giant ones?"

"Only if they admit that their bikes have both bodies and souls, and talk to their bikes." Peter flashed the famous Montpetit grin. "Hey, whatever the situation calls for, junior guides Jake Evans and Peter Montpetit rise to the occasion," he added, flexing a bicep and whipping the sofa's blanket over his shoulders like a cape.

"Does that mean you guys are going to blow everyone away at the motocross race this weekend?" Levi asked as his fingers reached into the popcorn bowl just before Peter's for the last handful.

Jake frowned into the fireplace as its burnt log collapsed into a glowing pile of embers. "I doubt Sergei will let us go anywhere till we help the Forest Service clear the mudslides off the trails. And there's not much chance of that by the weekend."

Everyone went quiet until Peter snapped his fingers. "Hey, I know where we can get a full-sized tractor and some free manpower to help us."

"Free manpower?" Jake asked, sneering at his buddy.

"Free boy-power. The Batemans."

"Who are the Batemans?" Jerry asked.

"Uh, some neighbors who offered to help Jake and

Peter around the ranch sometime," Levi assured his father, winking at Peter and Jake when his dad wasn't looking. "You know, I could always help, too, if Dad will let me stay some extra days."

"Sure you can stay on if it's okay with Sergei," Jerry said, yawning and standing up. "But I'm ready for bed. And I suspect Jake and Peter are more than ready for shut-eye."

"You betcha," Peter said. "Gotta get some sleep so we have tons of energy the next few days for clearing the trails. We'll load the llama cart up with shovels and get Salt and Pepper to help haul mud and rocks away. They're strong, those guys. Dana said they can pull their own weight, more than 300 pounds. And when we're done clearing the trails, we'll hit the motocross track and practise till …"

"Peter," Jake said, standing and pulling his buddy off the sofa by his T-shirt. "Jerry said shut-eye but he meant shut-mouth in your case."

"Oh. Okay then. Good night everyone."

24　The Team

Jake loved the smell of the pits. He loved the greasy, oily whiff of the machines up on their stands. He even loved the background noise on this brilliantly sunny Saturday noon in Spokane: the whine and roar of dirt bikes on the motocross track. He particularly liked having his favorite tools laid out within reach, maybe the way a surgeon likes his instruments laid out and ready as he scrubs up to perform an operation.

As he straightened up from doing a thorough suspension set-up on his bike, he also liked that a small circle of attentive motocross racers was gathered around him: Peter, Dana, Sergei, and the three Bateman brothers. After days of working together to clear the trails, and tons of after-hours spent riding the new whoops, the three ranch hands and their young neighbors were getting along.

Sergei, who didn't know the real reason the Bateman boys had "volunteered" to help out, had decided to thank them by loaning Chuck and Ian 125s just for this race. Martin Bateman had been so astonished by that loan, he'd been civil to the Back-of-Beyond group this morning, even bringing them doughnuts from the refreshment stand earlier. He was out along the fence watching the racers at the moment.

"So," Jake said, "before this afternoon's moto, I'd recommend everyone start by trying a compression dampening of two clicks and a return dampening of the same. Then you'll need to make final adjustments to your suspension. Unless, of course, you're on a factory team and have a wrencher who will do that sort of thing for you." He paused and looked directly at Peter. "But none of you are there yet."

"Not yet, so I'm told," Peter shot back with a ready grin.

"So, who remembers what I said about how to make dampening adjustments to the rear shock?"

"You need to use the special shock tool," Liam Bateman replied eagerly.

"That's right, Liam," Jake said, nodding at his favorite nine-year-old. He watched Dana hand Liam a felt-tipped pen and extend her cast arm for him to sign. "And what's the most important maintenance tip I've given you so far, Peter?"

"Clean your air filter," Peter responded, lying back in a camping chair and running a hand through his curls, trying to look bored. The façade didn't fool Jake. Peter was loving the fact that so far, he'd gotten all the answers right. In fact, Jake had been amazed how much information Peter could retain about maintenance, once his buddy put his mind to it.

"And make sure your rear chain is adjusted correctly," Chuck spoke up, face stern.

"Very good, both of you," Jake said, tapping his bike with his spark plug wrench the way a teacher might tap a blackboard with her chalk. "Okay, let's break it up and get ready for the afternoon's moto."

The boys immediately encircled Dana and got busy adding pictures to her arm cast, which was already colorfully crowded with signatures and drawings.

"Mudslide Mama," someone had scrawled in red.

"Dirt Diva," someone else had scribbled.

"All juniors in the 125 class to the starting line," the loudspeaker blared.

Jake's class sprang up as if a bell had rung.

"Hey, that includes Chuck and Ian today," Sergei said, resting his hands on the older Bateman brothers' shoulders. "Go hard. I'll be cheering for you."

"How come you're not racing?" Ian asked him.

"'Cause he's not supposed to for one week after a concussion," Dana spoke up.

"Nah, it's 'cause someone has to sweep and organize and cheer for you lot," Sergei corrected her, arms crossed over his barrel chest, "especially what with Dana's folks not being able to make it today."

Yeah, right, Jake thought, smiling. Or it means Sergei has some common sense after all. Five boys scattered to get their helmets, goggles, and gloves on. Dana, broom firmly in her left hand, watched them. She was wearing jeans and a form-fitting shirt that made her look, well, pretty good. Funny, Jake reflected, but he'd hardly ever seen her out of motocross gear.

"Want a lift?" he asked as he hopped on his motorcycle beside her. "Can't believe you aren't racing when Sergei said you could."

"Sergei's a vet, not a doctor, and last time I checked, I'm not a llama," she replied with a smirk. "I'm going to make sure my arm heals before I risk a fall. No, I don't need a lift, but you can walk your bike alongside me."

Jake got off to push his bike. He glanced down at her arm. "Couldn't be anyone at this race who hasn't signed that cast. And here I thought you were so shy you hardly talked with anyone."

Dana laughed and pointed the broom at him accusingly. "What's wrong with being shy?"

"Nothing, I guess. But I'm okay that you're not any more."

"Hmmm. Are you saying that, before you dug me out of the slide, I was a 'stick in the mud'?"

Now it was Jake's turn to laugh. Then he grew more serious. "So, eighteen guys in the 125 junior division today. Any tips for this afternoon's moto?"

"Mechanical or technique?"

"Body *and* soul, *gloopy*. Think I haven't figured out this week that I need both? Even Peter's come around to working on his own bike."

She paused and leaned on the broom with a contemplative look. She turned and gave him a warm smile.

"You're a born wrencher, Jake. Doesn't matter how you do in the motos. Just enjoy yourself. But," she paused for effect, "never give up. Anything can happen; anyone can go down last minute."

He should've pushed her for some real coaching tips. He should've felt let down, maybe even insulted. But as he made a face at her, and she made one back, Jake realized he felt good. She was right. He didn't need to prove anything on the course, only in the pits.

Twenty minutes later, Jake found himself beside Peter and Levi as the three revved their motors on the freshly swept pad.

"Go like stink!" Sergei delivered his usual line as he and Dana stepped back.

Jake gave them a thumbs-up and turned to extend it to Chuck and Ian. Then he addressed Peter.

"So, congrats again on taking the freestyle purse over halftime. I bet Honza's pretty mad about getting second."

"Probably, and thanks. I was counting on it, of course." Peter grinned his cocky grin but didn't turn his head. His eyes, Jake could see, were glued on the guy walking out onto the track with the thirty-second sign in his hand.

"Only 'cause you got lucky Dana couldn't compete," Jake teased him. The truth was, Jake was still stoked—and choked with worry—about having witnessed his buddy's perfect backflip.

"Not," Peter retorted, smiling. "I had lots of incentive, old buddy. I wanted that $100 to pay for pizza delivery up to Back-of-Beyond. Enough of cooking our own meals, I say!"

The guy with the thirty-second sign had changed it to five seconds, and before Jake could inform him that no pizza company was ever going to deliver to Back-of-Beyond, the gates dropped and he and Peter tore off. Jake was too far back to see Peter get the holeshot—become head of the pack—but far enough forward to be impressed with himself for being sure and steady so far. A number of laps later, Jake noted that Peter and Levi were in the lead, while The Brat in a yellow jersey and his hated rival Honza in red were not far behind. There was a definite gap between these four frontrunners and the rest of the pack. Chuck and Ian, on the other hand, brought up the rear. To Jake's mind, they were looking a little dodgy on the jumps, but at least they were hanging in there.

Two laps later, Jake noticed The Brat moving up so close to Peter's and Levi's tails that the boys had to know he was there. Honza, meanwhile, was approaching The Brat's tail. Honza had placed first in the morning's moto, Peter second, The Brat third, and Levi fourth.

"So, the yellow-jerseyed Brat thinks he can beat Peter this race, does he? I don't like the color yellow," Jake said to himself, eyes narrowing as he thought about how the llamas would agree with him.

With The Brat and Honza only a few exhaust-puffs behind his friends' fenders, Jake could only imagine the pressure they must be under. When The Brat cut Levi off to pass him, Jake had a feeling the kid was going to tail Peter until the last lap, then try something nasty to pull ahead of him. Was Peter guessing the same thing? Could he keep it from happening?

Minutes later, as Jake powered out of a tight hairpin, he saw Chuck and Ian riding abreast as if they cared more about sticking together than placing in a certain way. He watched the two try to do whips as they flew over a jump, then actually manage to pass one racer with elbows out, using as much of the track as possible. Jake smiled to himself. Wouldn't want to get on their bad side. The sight prompted Jake to goose it because "enjoying himself," as Dana had put it, didn't include being beaten by ten- and eleven-year-olds.

On the front hairpin, The Brat, still shadowing Peter, hit a rock with his front wheel and almost went down, costing him precious seconds to regain control. This made Jake cheer silently as he himself took a different and faster line through the corner. Now Honza was running in third place behind Peter and Levi, and The Brat was faced with fighting his way back from sixth. From well back in the pack, Jake watched the boy start to crash the berms and take corners and jumps at a crazy speed.

"Not a great strategy to count on blind luck," Jake thought. "And you're putting other riders in danger."

The bratty kid was brutally fast, no question. And the color of his jersey sure didn't match his level of determination. The next time the frontrunners passed Jake, churning earth into his face, The Brat had managed to work his way back to fourth position, beginning to close in on Honza and the still leading duo of Peter and Levi.

Jake watched, all but open-mouthed, as The Brat drew closer to Honza, coming into the hairpin recklessly fast. A split second later, Jake felt himself wince as The Brat slammed into the side of Honza, almost knocking him off his bike. Jake knew it was deliberate; The Brat used the collision to square off the corner and pass Levi. Jake's jaw loosened, and his blood began running red-hot. Had no one seen that dirty move? Was no official going to black-flag this guy, forcing him off the track immediately? Jake looked around to see who'd witnessed the attack. From the corner of his eye he noticed the Batemans, still riding tightly beside each other, jerk their heads in The Brat's direction. Jake wondered how many lap-counts the farm boys were behind the frontrunners.

The Brat, meantime, was gaining steadily on Peter. "The frontrunners are going to lap the Batemans right before the finish line," Jake thought. "Brat-Boy, you mess with Peter and you just might have to deal with the Bateman brothers. Trust me, you don't want to deal with the Bateman brothers."

As the Batemans came down the front straight heading for the last corner before the finish line, they were the only two riders separating Peter and Levi from The Brat and Honza, Honza having done an impressive recovery to regain fourth. Peter, Levi, The Brat, and Honza had let out all the stops at this point; they were going for the checkered flag.

At the final corner before the finishing jump, Ian Bateman took the berm on the outside of the corner. That's when The Brat tried the same dirty move he'd pulled off earlier, aiming to bank off Ian. But this time, Chuck seemed to anticipate what was about to unfold. He came into the corner fast on the inside. So fast he used up the entire track trying to make it. The Brat slammed right into the back of Chuck's bike before he had a chance to touch Ian. Jake smiled as the aggressor went down.

Amazingly Chuck's bike stayed upright, veering drunkenly back to the middle of the track; the bump from The Brat had only made him exit the corner with a bit more speed. As Chuck and Ian crested the jump right before the finish line, Jake saw the two boys exchange a mid-air high-five. Although Jake couldn't see from his position, he took that to mean the boys were seeing Peter crossing the finish line in first place, with Levi airborne right behind him.

Jake still had several laps remaining. On the next one, The Brat, he noted with satisfaction, was still sidelined trying to straighten his handlebars. Yet another lap later, he was still there, kicking the bike. Clearly, it wouldn't start.

"Even the Batemans might beat him now," Jake mused.

"Go like stink, Jake!" he thought he heard Sergei shout in his direction. And he did. Not because it made much difference whether he passed a bike or two, but because he wanted to get across that finish line for Peter and Levi's celebration. He wanted to join in Peter's hyper-dance, pump Levi's hand, and, when Chuck and Ian arrived, clap them on their backs, even if they shouldn't have done what they did.

"Come on, bike, do what you're made for," he growled at the machine beneath him as he gave it more throttle.

He hardly noticed roaring past one, then two competitors. When the checkered flag came down for him, he circled around and sped toward his pit fast. He had to veer to keep from hitting Dana when she broke away from the group and came running toward him, face shining. He hadn't even cut his motor before she'd given him a quick hug, her arm cast pressing roughly against his neck. Jake felt his face turning the same shade of red as the jersey of the third-place finisher, Honza Vozanilek.

Peter and the Batemans, even their father, were quick to gather around Jake on his bike.

"You placed twelfth, old buddy," Peter said, slapping him on the back. "That's much better than your first moto. And way to not be dead last, Chuck and Ian."

At this, Chuck guffawed. "Like second- and third-to-last is okay."

"Of course it's okay!" Sergei said. "It's your first 125 race, with bikes you'd never even tried out before!"

"Good enough for me," Martin Bateman said, his grin revealing the gaps in his teeth.

"Just wait till next time," Ian threatened, his effort at frowning failing to hide his lit-up eyes.

"Hey, what about me?" Liam asked, elbowing into the group. "I got fourth in my class."

"Excellent, Liam," Jake said, shaking the boy's hand.

Just then, Dana stuck the broom handle in front of Jake's face as if it were a microphone. "To what do you attribute your success, sir?" she panned like a reporter. Before he could answer, she swung the broom over to Peter and Levi. "And you two?"

"Well," Jake said, clearing his throat, rising from his motorcycle seat, and speaking into the broom, "I attribute it to keeping my body and soul in balance, and to talking to my motorcycle."

"Same," Peter intoned in a deep voice, face solemn.

Levi just chuckled and waved the broom away.

"*Da!*" Sergei cheered with a broad smile.

"Booo!" Chuck, Ian, and Liam mouthed between bouts of laughter.

"But mostly," Peter added, leaning closer to the broom handle and wiggling his eyebrows up and down at Dana, "I attribute it to the new factory team called Back-of-Beyond, and its awesome support network. Especially our sponsor, Sergei Dobrynina." He punched the shoulders of Jake, Levi, Chuck, Ian, Liam, and Sergei in turn.

"And your next goal?" Dana asked, mic still held up to Peter but eyes on Jake.

"To take up a new sport," Peter responded, leaning an elbow on Jake's shoulder. "Isn't that what we always do after acing the current one, Jake, my man?"

"That's the plan," Jake confirmed, daring to wink at Dana. "As soon as Sergei lets us out of harness."

Acknowledgements

Above all, I would like to thank Bill, Levi, and Nikki Lawrence of Kelowna, British Columbia, who adopted me on their motocross race circuit (which included Spokane, Washington). They put up with me trailing them with notebook in hand, and even invited me to spend time at the motocross track on their ranch. (Their ranch dog, of course, is named Scout.) They also suggested plot twists, patiently answered many dirt-bike questions, and read the chapters as I churned them out.

Deep appreciation is also due former motocross Canadian national champion Ron Keys of Oshawa, Ontario, and his daughter-in-law Carrie-Lynn Keys, a teacher at nearby Bolton C. Falby School. Ron painstakingly read the entire manuscript, contributing his own writing talent to suggested corrections.

Pete Moffat, my "techie consultant" throughout this series, also answered many motorcycle maintenance questions.

Very special thanks to John, Iris, and Anthony Fulker of Salt Spring Island, British Columbia's Bullock Lake Farm Bed and Breakfast, and their llamas Amador, Maxwell (RIP), and Benji. I truly couldn't get enough of traipsing about their llama fields, watching llama-cart racing videos, and listening to their llama tales. I failed to get spit at, however.

Chris Fitzsimmons and Deb Tichler, both registered nurses willing to take on fictional clients, helped with information about diabetes and first aid. Ekaterina Emm double-checked my Russian.

Thanks to all the motocross racers in Spokane who hung around the Lawrence "pits" to amuse themselves by answering my questions.

I'd like to acknowledge Coco, the guard llama, whose heroic fight with an eagle saved a hen and rooster, as written up in *Countryside and Small Stock Journal*, July 1, 1997.

And finally, thanks to the usual suspects: my husband, Steve; my son, Jeremy; my friend, Julie Burtinshaw; my editor, Carolyn Bateman; each and every staff member of Whitecap Books; my literary agent, Leona Trainer; and my speaking-tour agent, Chris Patrick.

ISBN 1-55285-510-4

1 "Up shot the kayak into the air, only to perform a harrowing backflip. Shoved helmet-first into the center of the spinning cocoon, Peter had never felt a force so determined to pry him from his boat. Hanging upside down, gripping his paddle shaft with all his might, Peter waited, counted, and prayed."

Arch rivals and sometimes friends Peter and Jake are delighted to be part of a whitewater-rafting trip. But after a series of disasters leaves the group stranded in the wilderness, it's up to them to confront the dangerous rapids to search for help. This is the first title in the extreme outdoor sports series by Pam Withers.

Jake, Peter, and Moses are looking forward to heli-skiing and snowboarding in the backcountry near Whistler. But just after they're dropped off on a mountain peak, bad weather closes in and a helicopter crashes. It's up to them to rescue any survivors and overcome avalanches, hypothermia, and wild animals to make their way to safety. This is the second title in the extreme adventure fiction series by Pam Withers.

ISBN 1-55285-530-9

ISBN 1-55285-604-6

It's summer vacation for best friends Peter and Jake, and when they're invited to help develop a mountain-bike trail west of the Canadian Rockies, they can't believe their luck. But as they start working hard in an isolated park, the boys sense that something's not right. Join the boys as they plunge into the mountain biking descent of their lives.

This is the third adrenalin-pumping outdoor sports adventure in the Take It to the Xtreme series.

3

Fifteen-year-olds Jake and Peter land jobs
as skateboarding stuntboys on a movie
set. The boys couldn't be happier, but
their dream job proves to be more trouble
than they expected. A demanding direc-
tor, an uneasy relationship with three local skateboarding toughs, and a sabotage
attempt—which suggests a jealous rival in
their midst—are just some of the obstacles
these stuntboys encounter. Coaching from
the town's new skate park manager—a
former X-Games champ—helps. But after
a police chase and an accident that lands
someone in the hospital, Jake and Peter
know it's time to find out who has it in for
them, and why!

ISBN 1-55285-647-X

Jake and Peter find extreme adventure once again. This time a scuba-diving accident leaves them and a surfer girl stranded on a deserted island with surfboards as their only means of escape. The storm of the century is fast approaching, and the boys need to think fast if they're going to get home in one piece. *Surf Zone* is Jake and Peter's most action-packed, thrilling adventure yet. This adrenalin-pumping book is sure to keep readers on the edge of their seats.

ISBN 1-55285-718-2

6

ISBN 1-55285-783-2

Jake and Peter stumble upon adrenalin-pumping adventure yet again, this time high in the peaks of the Bugaboo Mountains, just west of the Canadian Rockies. Fifteen-year-old Jake is obsessed with solo-climbing a soaring granite spire. His best friend Peter is as absorbed with filming Jake for a video as he is in not divulging his secret fear of heights to the runaway girl who joins them.

Packed with mountaineering lore and cliff-hanging tension, *Vertical Limits*, the sixth in the Take It to the Xtreme series, has competitive gym climbing, outdoor urban climbing, and wilderness rock climbing.